The Saint Mary's Horror

The Grey Girl, Book 3

The Saint Mary's Horror
The Grey Girl, Book 3

Copyright © 2019 by Shawn McLain

ISBN 978-1-7329408-0-2

Alistair's Return

Alistair coughed into the dank air of the abandoned building. Shivering against the cold, he cursed the darkness. Inhaling the stale musty air, he tried to take a deep calming breath. He coughed again as he attempted to focus his mind. Frustration overtook him as his mind wandered while he tried silently chanting a spell. He hadn't had to focus on a spell for decades. Cursing again, he re-focused his thoughts. A fire ignited in the long-forgotten grate. Alistair whooped in triumph, sending several rats skittering. His moment of victory drained in an instant as the truth of his surroundings became illuminated by the fire.

"I was *this* close," he exclaimed bitterly, holding his thumb and forefinger a fraction apart in front of the sightless eyes of the smiling woman in the crumpled magazine. "That damned girl and her demon friends ruined everything."

He smoothed out the picture. Focusing his energy, he stuck the picture to the wall. "Well, my dear, you will get to witness my return to power." Even as he spoke, exhaustion began to overwhelm him.

"Rest, that is what I need. Escaping from hell is quite tiring, you know." Alistair pulled his filthy cloak around him and curled, catlike, in front of his fire.

He was fighting against the tentacles streaming up from the pit. The noxious fumes of sulfur and death assaulted his senses. Alistair awoke tangled in his cloak. He was aware of the pitiful room, an awful stench, and a growling stomach.

It took him a moment to realize the eyes of the model were not the only ones watching him.

"Pretty neat trick with the fire there," wheezed a croaky voice.

Gagging slightly, Alistair covered his nose and pulled himself into a seated position. His bones ached with stiffness from the hard floor. His magic was another thing entirely. He could feel the return of power.

"I've been here for three days," the toothless mouth laughed, "and I ain't had to add nothing to it to keep it going." Alistair felt in his pockets as subtlety as he could while still trying to keep the stink from his nose.

"Oh, right." The man across from Alistair began to shuffle a bit, then produced from inside his tattered overcoat Alistair's watch and wallet. "Thought you was a corpse at first. Then I noted you was breathing." Again, he let loose a wheezing laugh. "You must be hungry. How long you been crashing here?" he asked, pulling a couple of label-less cans from his pockets. "Oh, they call me Sal. And you?" He held out a gnarled claw of a hand.

"Alistair," he said as he took he proffered hand, trying to hide his disgust. Sal either did not notice or care, or he was just used to this reaction.

"Well, Al, I hope it is okay with you if I share some floor and your amazing fire," Sal rambled, not paying much attention to what Alistair was doing. He just cozied up to the fire as he again rummaged in his pockets. Sal's tongue stuck out of the corner of his mouth as he pulled out crumpled rags, bits of paper, a few coins, and a bottle. He licked his lips, then opened the bottle, taking a long pull from it. His face screwed up in discomfort before he shook it away and offered the bottle to Alistair.

"Thank you, no." Alistair smiled coldly, waving away the inexpensive booze.

Shrugging off the refusal, Sal took another long swig. This time cocking his head to the side as he swallowed, his face returned to the grimace before he shook it free and placed the bottle close to his feet. "Right, don't want to drink on an empty stomach."

He was fumbling in his pockets again. This time he produced a rusting can opener. "Let's see what delicacies we have this evening." He giggled.

Alistair sat watching the old homeless man prepare a meal of ravioli and beans.

"House specialty," he proclaimed, "outdated mystery can delight." He laughed as he handed a battered and chipped mug of the cold mixture to Alistair.

They sat in silence for a time, Alistair thinking the entire time about restoring his magic. It took a few moments for him to realize that Sal was talking to him. "So, like I was saying," Sal repeated when he realized he had Alistair's attention, "you ain't heard nothing weird since you been here, have ya?"

"I'm sorry, what do you mean?" Alistair asked politely.

"Well, you see…" Sal began nervously. He took another drink. Then he seemed to be thinking. Alistair waited, allowing the other man to decide. Sal didn't look over at Alistair as he seemed to come to a conclusion. "I have been on the road for a while, traveling from place to place. About a week ago, I found a place to crash. This old hospital outside of town." Alistair's attention began to wane. Sal didn't notice. He was staring into the fire. "The place was what you would expect. Junkies, kids partying. It had seen better days." He threw some of the bits of paper from his pocket into the flames.

"At first the noises didn't bother me. Old place, you know, not alone in there." He shuddered. "But that wasn't all. One night I heard a girl talking." He glanced at Alistair. "I know what you are thinking. Teenagers and such—but there was something different about this young girl's voice. She was angry. She didn't want us there." Alistair was watching Sal closely. Sal turned to look into Alistair's eyes. Fear radiated from him. "That place was haunted. It wasn't just the girl, although," he shuddered, "she was horrible, screaming and screeching." Sal stared into the flames, and the corner of his eye twitched as if he could still hear the screaming. "No, there was something far worse. One of the other guys started screaming back at her, and that is when it happened." Alistair waited. Sal didn't seem to want to continue. The memories sent anguish across his face. "I thought we were going to die."

Disappointed, and with a growing loss of patience, Alistair glared at the stricken man. "Some little girl's ghost scared you that badly?" Alistair spat, "Pathetic."

"She was terrifying in her anger; you weren't there."

"I have faced off with far worse than little ghost girls. I have seen demons. Faced them, fought them, and defeated them. I have tricked them into doing my bidding, I have taken their…" Alistair faltered, realizing Sal was not listening to him. Instead, he was curled up in the corner hugging himself and rocking back and forth, his hands clamped tightly over his ears. Somewhere in the distance, a dog was howling.

Sal was weeping. "The wolf," he whispered, "can you hear the wolf?" He pointed to a dingy, loosely boarded up window. Ugly yellow tungsten lighting seeped around the poorly attached boards. "It's after me!" Sal grabbed Alistair by the shoulders, shaking him. All sanity had fled his eyes, replaced by manic terror. "It knows. It wants me dead. I should have never stepped foot into its lair." He dissolved into frightened weeping. Alistair pushed him away in disgust.

"You were run off by a dog, you fool."

"This was no dog!" Sal sprang to his feet, his hands balled into fists. "I know dogs! This was a wolf, damn it."

"There are no wolves here." Alistair had tired of the conversation. He debated in his mind the best way to dispose of this foul-smelling man. "I could just disintegrate him," he whispered, "no muss, no fuss, no cleanup." He laughed silently.

"A wolf, you hear me?"

"Oh, good lord, he's still ranting?" Alistair moaned, starting to conjure the blue-green flame he would use to destroy his companion. The energy fizzled and died at Sal's next words.

"It was a demon wolf, spectral and huge!" Sal's arms flew wide, "Big enough to swallow a man whole."

"A demon wolf, you say?" Alistair asked quietly.

"Yes! Haven't you been listening?" Sal shouted. Now it was Alistair's turn to grab Sal by the shoulders. Fire glinted in his eyes that turned Sal's anger to trepidation. "it was huge and it chased us out," Sal finished quietly.

"You found this in an abandoned hospital, not far from here, you say?" Alistair's grip on Sal grew tighter. Sal nodded, and his heart began to pound painfully against his ribs.

Alistair's face loomed closer as he said, "You will take me there."

Sal's protests died, as did his desire to run. The issues that had sent him on his long journey of alcohol and wandering disappeared. He only wanted, only needed, to get his master to the hospital. They needed to retrace his steps to where he had seen the giant ghost wolf.

Should I Buy a Van?

"Come on, Chloe," Alex called, "there is nothing here." He was standing on the rickety porch of an old abandoned farmhouse. "The only thing in this place are bugs and mice," he muttered.

"If it is only mice, why are there so many stories?" Chloe called from near the dilapidated barn.

"How in the hell does she hear that?" Alex whispered.

"*Language,*" she called over her shoulder, "and I hear everything." She flashed the smile that allowed her to get away with almost anything. "And I hear something in the barn."

Shaking his head and shrugging, he stepped off the termite eaten step onto the overgrown grass. "Probably just flies fu…"

"Alex!" Chloe spun to glare at him. "That is not the type of word we use in polite company."

"Oh my god, Chloe, you are such an old woman sometimes." He laughed, but he quickly swallowed his mirth. Now she wore the look that told him he had really stepped in it.

"I may look young and vibrant—I *am*—but I still retain the sensibilities of my time." Her hands had found her hips as her eyes burned into his, the stars reflected in the black of her pupils. "Your generation just has no manners, no sense of decorum. Alex, are you even listening to me?" Those eyes had captivated him again. Now that he could see the flames behind them, he took a step back.

"What? Sorry, honey, I was…" He tried to explain, but his attention was snagged by something behind Chloe.

"Don't 'honey' me." Her tone shifted at the look on his face. "Alex, what is it?" She turned slowly to see a mist creeping slowly out of the barn. As they watched, it began to take shape. A hulking mass that was forming taut muscle slowly materialized. It was a spectral horse, adorned with a skeletal mount. The skeleton wore a shabby uniform that flowed in a non-existent breeze. Alex stood shaking in fear, as Chloe huffed. "Come on out," she called. Red eyes glowed on the horse and fire burst from its mouth as it reared up. Alex tried to grab Chloe's shoulder to pull her back. She shrugged him off to stand under the beast's massive hooves.

"Chloe!" His hissed warning received only a wave off from Chloe. Her hands were back on her hips, and Alex knew her face was set in determination.

"I said," her voice was strong and determined, "enough of this, and come out!" The horse and rider vanished.

A small voice called from the barn. "He'll come to find me!" Worry carried on the wind.

"Who is coming?" Chloe asked, approaching the door slowly. Alex could see the face of a young boy, pale and ghostly, peeking out between the rotting wooden doors.

"He is." A transparent arm reached out from the darkness, its finger pointing back toward the house. Alex and Chloe turned to see a large angry-looking man bursting through the door. He was pulling his belt off as he marched to the barn. Chloe stepped into the path of the charging man. He stuttered to a stop, and confusion chased anger around his features. He starred in shock at Chloe.

"How?" was all the man could muster.

"Why are you going after that boy?" Chloe demanded.

The question seemed to puzzle the man for a moment. The anger returned as he attempted to push Chloe out of the way. "This is none of your concern, girl. That boy is stealing my milk!"

Even though his hand passed through Chloe, hers had stopped him, as solid as a rock. Before she could speak, the boy in the barn cried out.

"I didn't steal nothing!" Tears evident in his voice. "I am looking for my dog. A horseless carriage scared him, and he ran this way." The boy, no more than ten, stepped out, a pleading look on his face. "Please, sir, can you help me find him?" The man faltered, and he looked from the boy to Chloe and back.

"I didn't mean to," he said, dropping the belt. "I didn't know."

Alex approached slowly. The man's eyes spotted him moving toward the boy. "I heard someone in my barn. I thought it was a thief." Alex crouched by the boy, who was staring up at the man. "I threw open the door to startle them. I didn't know you were there." The man dropped to his knees.

The boy passed through Alex, approaching the now weeping man. "Mr. Baker?" The boy carefully touched the man's shoulder.

"I killed you," Mr. Baker wept. "I threw open the door. It smashed you in the head. You died right there." He was pointing to the entrance of the barn. "I didn't know what to do. I ran back to the house, but," his eyes went wide, "my chest hurt. It hurt so bad." He looked up Chloe, with pleading eyes.

"I'm so sorry; you died," Chloe explained.

"You come storming out every night," the boy whispered, "always so mad. I can feel the door," and he rubbed at a dark spot on his head.

"I am so sorry, so, so, sorry," Mr. Baker cried, taking the boy's hand. The child looked into the man's eyes and spoke.

"It was an accident. You didn't mean to."

Alex gasped, pointing at the front of the farmhouse. Mr. Baker turned, helped to his feet by the boy. "Rebecca," the man moaned.

"Oh, Hugh, it's been so long." The ghost of Rebecca smiled. Hugh Baker's spirit took one tentative step, then another. He crossed the distance at a run, taking up the woman in his arms. She laughed as he twirled her around.

Unseen by the reunited couple, the boy slipped his hand into Chloe's. He wore a sad smile. Hugh turned back with tears in his eyes.

"I have been trapped by guilt," he said. "I think I can leave now." He put the woman down, though she still held tight to his arm. "Boy, can you leave? I won't go if you can't leave too."

The child looked from the ghost couple to Chloe, "I don't feel no different. I don't think I can go." His words caused a moan of sadness and despair from Hugh. Over his cry, Alex heard something. Chloe and the boy heard it too.

"Is that a dog barking?" Chloe asked. From nothing, a terrier appeared.

"Ralphie!" the boy screamed, running to the dog. It leaped into his arms. He turned to the others, the brightest smile on his face. "He's come to take me home." He waved and vanished. Hugh was being hugged by Rebecca.

"Thank you for finally freeing them," Rebecca said as she and Hugh vanished into the mist.

Alex walked up to Chloe and pulled her into a one-armed hug. "You did good…" he smirked, "for an old lady."

She threw off his arm and slapped his shoulder. "Yaaga," she cried, and Alex's own shout echoed hers as they both shielded their eyes from bright headlights.

A door slammed and a shadow crossed in front of the lights. Aaron called from in front of the car, "Hey, what time is this haunting thing supposed to start?"

"Dude!" Alex shouted. "You missed it, again."

"Probably got too busy with his studies," Chloe whispered, making air quotes when she said "studies". Raising her voice, "You know, if you want to be part of the investigations, you need to start showing up on time." She grabbed Alex by the hand, pulling him toward her car. "Maybe you should bring her along next time," she suggested.

"Then what? I get a dog and a van?" Aaron grumbled.

"I guess that would make you Shaggy," Chloe laughed, shutting her door.

"Of all the cartoons, from all the years, she falls in love with that one." Aaron frowned. "I guess it is better than Smurfs." Aaron turned up his radio as he followed Chloe's headlights back to town.

Searching

Alistair's patience grew thin. He was tired, but try as he might, the back of the sedan was not nearly as comfortable as he had been led to believe. He wanted to make the shaggy, flea filled head of the driver explode. The only thing keeping him alive was the fact that Alistair had no idea where the hospital was. Although the longer they drove, the less confident he was that Sal knew either.

"I am beginning to wonder," Alistair snarled, "if this wolf of yours was nothing more than a drunken delusion." He began to play with a few flames in his hand, flicking them onto the seat. As each left a small round hole in the fabric, he imagined Sal's screams as he flicked the same fire onto his face. Alistair's shoulders shot up to his ears as he heard Sal's wheezing laugh.

"Oh no master, it was real." Sal seemed to be getting excited. "The place was filled with ghosts and creatures. I remember the girl now, and there were some weird beast-men and all kinds of things floating around."

"I know someone who will be a ghost if we do not get there soon."

Sal seemed happy with the threat. "Oh Master, I recognize this area." He slowed in front of a graffiti-covered house. "I spent a night or two here." He pointed a gnarled hand at the black hole where the front door had once been. "This is a good place to spend the night," he announced happily.

Alistair had reached his limit. Summoning his anger, he prepared to vaporize his useless minion. He froze at the tapping on the window. A heavy black metal flashlight was rapping against the glass next to his driver. Before Alistair could say a word, Sal clicked the button to roll down the window. "Good evening." A light shone in Alistair's eyes. Behind him, red and blue began to flash as another flashlight bounced closer to the car. "May I ask what you two are doing here?"

Alistair assessed the situation and was about to answer. He slapped his forehead when Sal answered. "Oh, I thought my Master would be tired, so I suggested we sleep here. You see, I slept here a few nights ago." He smiled his green-toothed grin at the officer. "I was running for my life, you see." Alistair opened one eye to see the other policeman looking at him, his hand on the butt of his service weapon. "See, I had been crashing at this abandoned hospital when this huge ghost wolf came after me." Sal's attention turned from one officer to the other, a giant stupid smile plastered on his face. "I told Master about the wolf and he wants to see it for himself. So that is where we are going." Sal's smile slipped. "Except I don't remember exactly where it was. Do you know where we can find an abandoned hospital with a huge ghost wolf?"

"Step out of the car, please," the officer by the door commanded, opening the door for Sal. "You too," he motioned to Alistair. "Do either of you have any identification?" Sal happily patted his pockets and began to pull out a wide assortment of items, placing them on the hood. Alistair kept his hands in sight and shook his head at the question. "I assume you have a reason you are driving around a known crack house in a stolen car?" the officer asked. Alistair closed his eyes, readying his magic.

"Oh, weren't you listening?" Sal asked. "I stole the car on Master's orders, to look for the old hospital, and I thought this would be a good place to sleep for the night."

"So, you knew the car was stolen. You admit you are the one who stole it." The officer asked in disbelief.

"Of course, we needed it, just like we needed money." Sal pulled out a wallet, and then another. This one was a woman's. Sal leaned in, covering the side of his mouth conspiratorially. "I had to kill this couple to get it." He winked and laughed.

Alistair moaned. Two guns were drawn while the police shouted orders. Sal did not respond. Alistair concentrated. Sal jumped on the officer. He was biting and clawing at the man. Two shots rang out, and Sal fell dead. The bleeding cop looked up to his partner. Alistair laughed as the gratitude slipped away, turning to fear. Two more shots rang out. The officer fell, blood streaming from the wounds in his head. The radio called for the officers. The lone officer lowered his gun and bowed slightly to Alistair.

"Now that the annoyances are out of the way," he glanced at the two bodies, "Officer Jones, do you know where I can find an abandoned hospital?"

"Yes, sir, that would be Saint Mary's. I'll take you there." He walked back to the cruiser and held the passenger door open for him. Alistair slid in behind a computer screen. A grin spread across his face as the officer pulled away. The emergency lights were flipped off, as was the radio. Alistair began to type a name into the computer. *Chloe Miller.*

Searching, the Other Side

"Hey Chlo, what are we doing?" Aaron asked, looking up from his laptop screen.

"Not watching videos," Alex stated, clicking Aaron's mouse. "We told you, we are looking for any sign of Alistair." Grabbing a coffee, he was about to ask Chloe if she wanted one when a mug scraped along the counter. The coffee decanter tipped to pour a cup, when another skidded up, knocking the first cup out of the way. Aaron grinned mischievously at Chloe. She raised an eyebrow at him. A smoke-like creature landed lightly on the counter. Aaron half rose from his chair. The ghost cat turned to him, lay on his coffee cup, then disappeared, taking the cup with it. Chloe waved her hand and her cup filled and floated to her.

"I really don't think that is what Liza had in mind when she started training you," Chloe laughed, raising her cup to him. Aaron cried out as the ghost cat materialized on the table in front of him with a full cup of coffee. It was not the same cup though.

"Well, she would not have sent this if she was upset." Aaron returned her salute. Behind them, Alex grumbled about having to fetch his own drinks. Aaron and Chloe shared a laugh. Coming around the table, Alex looked at Chloe's screen.

"I'm sorry, Aaron. Apparently, we are not searching for a crazed murderous wizard. We are instead," he spun her computer so Aaron could see the screen, "looking at vacation sites."

"Or honeymoon," Aaron muttered, earning a glare from Chloe. "Forgot about super ghost girl ears," he barely whispered. This did not endear him any further with her.

"Enough… do I have to separate you two?" Alex sat down and sipped his coffee as he opened his computer. "Come on, Aaron you check these sites. Chloe here is yours, and I'll take these." He ignored his fiancé and brother calling him 'dad.' The next half hour, the only sounds to be heard were the clicking of keys, the purr of real and ghost cats, and the occasional exclamation that turned to disappointment. Finally, Alex groaned as he rubbed his eyes. "This is hopeless." Stretching, he let his head fall back, arms out above his head. "I don't even know what I am looking for."

"This," Chloe stated. She spun her screen so they could see. The report was about a murdered couple.

"I am not seeing it," Alex sighed. "Looks like they were mugged." He pulled the computer closer. "See? Money taken, knife wounds." He continued to read, "Witnesses said they were attacked by a couple of homeless men. No, wait." Alex pulled the computer closer, reading the article more closely. Aaron looked from one to the other expectantly. "Oh, oh wow," Alex breathed.

"Got there, did you?" Chloe smiled.

"Oh yeah."

"You two mind letting the rest of the class in on it, then?" Aaron pouted.

"The article covers the murder," Chloe started, "but there are some weird inconsistencies in the witness statements."

"One said there were two assailants," Alex interrupted, "but it was just the one doing the stabbing. While the woman was being killed her husband just stared blankly ahead. He then handed over his wallet and let the man stab him eighteen times."

Chloe jumped in, "One witness said it was like both the man and the killer were in a trance. The only one who seemed to know what was going on was the other homeless man." She paused as a smile spread across her face, "A homeless man in a cloak. A cloak with burns!" she exclaimed triumphantly.

"Um, ok, a bum in a burnt bathrobe. Not seeing the connection to our evil wizard," Aaron said.

"Oh my god!" Chloe shouted, "Are you sure you are brothers?" she demanded of Alex.

"Damn, Chlo, relax—I was just kidding." Aaron defended. "Where did this happen?

"Some town near State College," Alex replied, "a couple of hours east."

"That is a lot of ground to cover," Chloe groaned.

"And the only way we can find out where he is, is to wait for more bodies to show up." Alex rubbed his eyes again and ran his fingers through his hair in frustration. "Unless…" but his thought was immediately shouted down. They were not going to call upon Kerlvin to help.

"Maybe Liza can find him?" Aaron asked hopefully. A second after he said it, an attractive red-haired woman appeared, leaning against the kitchen counter and sipping a cup of fragrant tea.

"I told you, he has cloaked himself from me." Liza shrugged. "But it is nice you think I can change that fact in twelve hours. Honestly, darling, you need to listen and hear what I am saying." She leaned over to give Aaron's cheek a tweak. Alex made a gagging noise that caused Chloe to laugh, then she tried to play it off as a cough. Liza ignored all of it. "But since we know an approximate location, I might be able to trace his magic if we get close enough.

New Home

Alistair waved his hands, sending loose boards and chains flying. A set of doors swung wide as if they were welcoming him in. "Yes, yes, this will do nicely." He inhaled deeply, "Yes, I smell…" He sniffed again. Holding his hands out to feel the air, his crooked smile grew, "At least a dozen souls here." His face switched to anger in an instant. The police officer had just tripped, sending a rickety table onto its side. Several bottles shattered and cans rattled across the filthy entry. "Idiot!"

The officer looked like a two-year-old who didn't understand he had done something wrong. He smiled blankly at Alistair. "This place could use a good cleaning." The policeman shrugged. Alistair felt the anger and the power start to build in his hands. He quickly squelched his magic. The vibrations in the air told him something was watching. He could hear their whispered conversations. They knew he was something different, and they were afraid. The crooked smile returned.

"Yes, perhaps you could tidy up a bit," Alistair mused. The officer immediately began to remove the accumulated detritus of decades. A satisfied smirk lay on his face as he watched the man pick up broken glass and get stuck by used needles and yet not seem to notice. The hissed whispers of the inhabitants pleased Alistair. Moving further into the lobby he waved his hands, sending more dirt flying. An ancient half circle couch righted itself, stuffing returned to the cushions, stains lifted and evaporated, the stitching mending itself in seconds. Alistair moved around the now pristine piece of furniture. Its deep burgundy color pleased him, as did its velvet feel. Flopping down on the couch like it was a throne, he threw his arms wide on the back of the couch. "Yes, this will be quite lovely when I am finished." Another wave of his hand cleared the area around him of filth and decay.

"Um, Master?" a voice called from behind the couch. Alistair ignored it. "Um, sorry to bother you, but…" Alistair's fingers found his temples as he sighed in frustration. Turning around he glared at the policeman. "Sorry, but I appear to be bleeding rather badly."

Alistair jumped. It was rare that he could be surprised. A new voice spoke from Alistair's shoulder. "Well, that does seem to be a problem." Alistair spun to face the owner. Another rarity occurred as Alistair sprang away. Standing there was something out of a nightmare or a horror movie. Something that Alistair could not immediately understand or believe. Under a filthy tattered doctor's coat, covered in worn trousers, a moth-eaten sweater, and frayed tie and collar, stood a skeletal corpse. The eyes were bright and alert behind round wire-rimmed glasses. The face was gaunt and grey, the hair white and thinning. Discomfort rode up Alistair's spine as the creature moved toward the policeman, its bones grinding loudly as it walked. Oddly, its stride was long and even. The desiccated hands took the officer's and began to examine them. "Oh, this will require some stitches," it spoke, "good thing I am a doctor, wouldn't you say?" It turned to Alistair and winked.

Shaking himself off, Alistair found his voice and his feet. "That will not be necessary." The corpse doctor raised a dusty white eyebrow at this. "Officer," Alistair faltered, not remembering the man's name. Shrugging it off, he continued, "Officer, take that infernal car of yours, drive many miles away from here, and when the fuel begins to get low, drive as fast as you can into a house." Alistair waved the man away. Satisfied, he turned to glare at the doctor.

"Oh, bravo, bravo!" The walking corpse applauded, and dust rose from his hands as they slapped together, muted like the applause of gloves. "Makes things easier, doesn't it?" He smiled, exposing gree- grey teeth. His interest was drawn to the blood on his hands. Alistair involuntarily drew back as the doctor sucked the blood from his fingers. The look on his face showed the relish he had for the taste. "Oh, where are my manners?" Alistair feared the creature was going to offer a bloody finger to suck on as it held out a hand. "Doctor Phineas Pryor," he gave a slight bow, "at your service."

Tentatively Alistair took the proffered hand, "Alistair." He grimaced, feeling the brittle bones under the leathery skin shift under his grasp.

"Pleasure," Dr. Pryor grinned. "I have the feeling you and I are going to get along swimmingly." The grin caused a sensation Alistair hadn't felt in decades. If he remembered correctly, it might have been fear. "Please follow me. There is much I want to show you." Dr. Pryor walked to a set of shattered glass doors, and holding one open, he extended his arm, beckoning Alistair to follow.

1952

The snow had come early that year. The children's ward was decorated with happy pumpkins and cute black cat cutouts. Orange and black paper chains hung on the metal bed headboards. Orderly William Red Horse smiled sadly at the room as he finished his rounds. The curtains were pulled between the beds for a bit of privacy. Most of these children would never leave this ward. Billy, as everyone called him, knew that. Many were polio victims, some had other debilitating illnesses, but all were orphans. Billy felt a connection to them, as he had lost his family when he was still quite young. His mother and father had met at the Carlisle Indian School. It was their experiences there that had led to his father's alcoholism, followed by his mother's suicide. Billy shook the anger away as he slowly let the door shut silently on the room. He glanced one last time at the ten occupied and two unoccupied beds. He hoped they would stay that way until after Christmas.

His shift was almost over as he headed toward the emergency entrance. He always stopped in to chat with Reginald, the night watchman. Billy and he would often joke about how, if there was a problem, Reggie could do nothing about it. Wounds he had collected in the war kept his mobility very limited. "Still," he would say, "at least the head doctor allows me to keep working. After I came back, he insisted I take my old job back."

"Yeah, I was just training as a medic in Korea when I got hit and sent home," Billy unconsciously rubbed his upper thigh. There were still nights he pulled shrapnel out of the huge scar that had taken out a large chunk of muscle. "I was offered a job here while I was still recovering at the VA."

Reggie lit up a cigarette and squinted through the smoke to the swirling snow. Billy saw it too; a flashing red light, barely visible through the heavy blizzard. "Damn it," Reggie swore as another light joined the first, then a third. Pushing himself up, he moved as fast as his damaged body would allow. Without a word, Billy sprinted to the nurses' station.

The first ambulance had already arrived when Billy returned to help Reggie with the doors. The ambulance staff was busy with a plunger and mask contraption, trying to force air into the lungs of a patient. Reggie shook his head sadly. The second ambulance pulled up and a gurney was rushed in. Billy's heart ached as he saw the small frame of a young woman, her face and clothes covered in blood. The next gurney he saw broke his heart. The wind whipped the red-stained sheet off the head of another young woman. "A blessing in disguise." Reggie shuddered. Seeing Billy's confused and demanding eyes, he placed a hand on his shoulder. "There was so little left, she was practically cut in half." Finally, the third and final ambulance arrived.

Billy shivered from the cold wind, and the lack of urgency of the ambulance crew. He hurried to the back of the third ambulance, ready to lend a hand. "Sorry, Billy, but there is no hurry. She didn't make it," a gruff man spoke as he opened the back door. Billy could make out the shape of a woman under the sheet. He could tell certain limbs were not attached.

"What happened?" Billy asked. Reggie was hobbling out with a jacket for Billy. They followed the body into the hospital. A nurse handed out coffee to the ambulance crew and Reggie. She sniffed with disdain at Billy. She walked away grumbling when Reggie forced his coffee into Billy's shaking hands. Another nurse walked up to the men.

"The man didn't make it," she sighed, and she handed Reggie a fresh cup of coffee. She looked down the hall. "That poor girl, she's lost her whole family in one night."

"What… what happened?" Billy whispered.

"Whiteout conditions," explained a policeman. Billy hadn't noticed the officer's arrival. He was never comfortable around police. "From what we can tell—thank you," someone handed him a coffee, "The man was driving and didn't see the tight curve on 59 and went over the side." He blew on the coffee. "No idea how long they were there before someone noticed. The car was partially covered, and the wife and one of the girls were already dead when we got there."

A doctor Billy didn't recognize walked up. "The man didn't survive," he told the officer.

"Damn," the policeman muttered, pushing his hat off his forehead.

"How is the other girl?" Billy asked quietly.

The doctor stared at Billy as if he was seeing him for the first time. It seemed like he was trying to understand the question. "Oh, her," he finally responded, not looking Billy in the eye, "She'll live, but it might have been better for her if she hadn't. I doubt she'll ever leave here." Billy felt the anger burn in the pit of his stomach. How would it be better for her to die? The doctor rubbed the back of his head as he blew out a long, exhausted breath. "She was the reason they were out on a night like this. She is very sick." He still couldn't meet Billy's eyes. "We don't expect her to recover." He turned his back on the group. "In fact, I doubt she will make it to Christmas."

A nurse was wheeling out a gurney. Billy could see the young woman's face now. It was bruised and scraped and bandaged. Billy thought it a shame that one so young would be taken so soon. He walked up to the girl's side. Taking her hand, he whispered, "I'll make sure you are happy and comfortable as long as I can." He jumped back from the girl as a shadow fell over her.

"That is very noble of you," smiled the chief surgeon. "I think we may be able to see this young lady leave this hospital." The other doctor sputtered with incredulous frustration. The chief surgeon raised his hand to calm his subordinate as he looked over the chart. "Ms. Norah Sheppard, sixteen years old." Billy looked down at the girl.

She was so tiny, he couldn't believe she was that old. The doctor continued, "I was waiting for her to arrive. We have some new treatments for her condition." He inspected the injuries. "Shame about her family." He looked up at Billy, who was trying not to be noticed. "I believe you will be the one." He handed the clipboard to the other doctor.

"The one, sir?" Billy asked.

"Yes, you will be the one she will be doing her rehabilitation with. William," Dr. Pryor smiled at Billy, "Meet your new friend and ward, Norah Sheppard."

Other Business

Alex sat on the couch, rubbing his eyes with one hand while petting Fear the cat with the other. Aaron and Liza had gone home, and Chloe had run out to pick up something for dinner. He was tired. Dealing with the haunting the night before, then searching through the weirder side of the internet, had worn him out. He let his hand fall to the arm of the couch while still feeling the rumbling purr of the cat as he continued his rhythmic petting. Without warning, the purring was replaced by a hiss and then the cat was gone. Alex did not lift his head or open his eyes at the sudden departure. "Silly cat," he mumbled as light tendrils of sleep began to envelop his mind.

Instantly he was awake and alert. Staring around the room, he felt his heart slamming against his chest. He had not heard a sound, but he was terrified. The room was like ice; small puffs of breath formed from his rapid breathing. All of the color seemed to drain from the room until he was looking out a window he did not recognize. He became aware he was no longer alone. Not wanting to look but unable to stop, he slowly turned his head toward his companion. She was barely five feet tall and very thin. She looked like a fragile doll, but her eyes told of someone older. She was staring at him if she was surprised. She looked slightly confused, unsure why he should be there.

Alex opened his mouth to ask who she was when she quickly silenced him. "Shhh," she quietly hissed, holding a finger to her lips, "death is coming." She began to move, catlike, and swiftly down the carpeted room toward a set of glass doors. Alex took another glance out the window and realized he could see almost nothing through them. Looking back to his companion, he noticed she had stopped and was gesturing for him to follow. "Hurry," she hissed, "death is coming."

Follow the strange girl, or wait for death? Hmmm. Alex pondered sarcastically before following. She passed through the doors to a long, curved hall. There were windows along one side, but again Alex could not see clearly what lay beyond. They passed through another set of doors. Alex lost sight of the girl for a second. A *psst* called from an open door, followed by a pale thin arm, beckoning. Alex stepped toward the darkness. A small hand reached out for his wrist and with a strength he did not expect, he was pulled into the shadows. His skin crawled under her icy hands, one now held his wrist and one covered his mouth. He began to protest only to hear her *shhhhhh* next to his ear. He was pulled down and further into the dark. Alex could now hear footsteps— muted, yet getting louder.

The tiny frozen hand slipped from his face. "Death is here," she breathed. Alex's heart raced and his shoulders tightened at the squeak of the heavy glass doors opening. The footsteps grew louder. Alex realized there was more than one set. Words were being exchanged between "Death" and someone else, and they were approaching the room. "Quiet! He will not stop if there is no sound," she instructed. Alex was sure the clamor of his heart would betray them; the blood was pounding in his ears. The icy hand returned to his lips as Alex gasped. A skeletal creature, dressed in tattered clothes, was passing smoothly in front of the open door. That was not what forced the sound from his lungs, though. Walking next to this walking cadaver was Alistair, the wizard they had been looking for.

Alex shut his eyes tight. This was a dream—he had fallen asleep on the couch, and this was a dream. The cold left his lips and wrist. He took that as a sign. "See, a dream, that's all," he mumbled, yet he was aware that he was crouched in a corner against a tiled wall that did not exist in their house. "Wake up, Alex, this is just a dream," he commanded.

"My name is not Alex," a whisper near him scolded.

Alex's eyes flew open. He was in the dark corner of an unfamiliar room staring out of a door into a dim hall. "Where the hell am I?" he demanded, searching the darkness for his companion.

"That is an astute assessment of the situation," was the reply. "Perhaps this is hell." The shadow of the girl stood in the doorway. "Not the biblical version, I admit." Her pale face was visible as she looked one way, then the other, down the hall. "I think they have gone to his office."

She turned back to him, holding out a hand. He ignored it, using the wall to push himself upright. If she was offended, she did not show it. "Come along, step lively. We need to get up to the third floor before they decide to come back." She took a few steps along the hall. Alex stuttered to a halt as she appeared to be blocking his exit. She pondered a moment, then whispered, "Or worse, he sends out the things."

She turned, moving briskly down the hall. Stunned it took Alex a moment to shake his head clear to follow. "Things? What things?" he hissed, sprinting to catch up. "Hey, what things?"

Disappearance

"Hey, you want to give me a hand?" Chloe called from the doorway to the garage. She held a grocery bag, a pizza, and a drink, all while trying to keep the door from swinging closed. "Alex!" she shouted again. "Fine, I'll just have to eat this entire thing by myself." Finally struggling through the door, she set the items down on the kitchen counter. Leaning over the back of the couch she expected to wake him up. He wasn't there. "Alex," Chloe called again, annoyance mixed with a feeling of dread. She checked their bedroom, the bathrooms, and even the basement. He wasn't there. She double-checked the counter and any other area he might have left a note. Next, she searched her phone for a message. There was nothing. She hit the call button under his picture and waited. She heard the muffled ringtone coming from the living room. Following it to the couch, she found the phone wedged between the cushions. Checking his phone, he had no recent calls and no texts. There was nothing that could explain where he was.

"He wouldn't have left this behind," she said to the ghost cat that sat in the corner grooming its tail. Just like a live cat, it ignored her. Chloe went outside and walked around the house. His car was in the garage, as was his bike. Nothing was out of place in the house. A feeling of panic began to burn in the pit of her stomach. "Ok, calm down," she told herself. She found Aaron's number and hit the button. Every ring was an eternity. "Pick up the damn phone, Aaron, pick up the phone!" She was pacing. It went to voice mail. Her cry of frustration fell on the deaf furniture. "You boys better be in trouble or you are seriously going to be!" she shouted into the phone after the beep. Holding both her phone and Alex's, she walked out the front door, down the walk, and out to the street. Sometimes Alex and she would go for a walk when it was nice out. Maybe he just went for a walk, she reasoned, staring down the long flat empty road. But with dinner on the way and without his phone?

Chloe squeaked in alarm when the phone vibrated and then burst into song. It took a second to determine whose phone it was. She saw the name and prayed Alex was standing right next to him.

"Damn, Chloster, what was with that message?"

"Is he with you?" she demanded.

"No!" came the angry reply. "Wait, I called his phone." His tone was now concerned. "Chloe, why do you have Alex's phone?"

Chloe fought to keep her emotions in check, but she was failing. "Aaron, I don't know where he is. I went out to get dinner and when I came back, he wasn't in the house. I found his phone in the couch and I've looked in every room, in the basement because we got that pool table, but wasn't there so I ran outside—I thought he might have taken a walk but... it doesn't make any sense."

She was rambling and realized Aaron was shouting her name. "Yes? Sorry." A tear ran down her cheek.

"Listen, I'm going to call Dad. Maybe he had an emergency and Alex left with him and forgot his phone." Aaron took a deep breath as Chloe fought a sob. "I know what you are thinking, and stop it," he chastised. "I'll call Liz and have her check the house for magic. If he isn't with Dad, I'll be over in like, ten minutes." Chloe was relaxing a little now that she had someone to talk to. Liza had warded the house; there was no way Alistair could have found them. "You said you picked up dinner?" Aaron asked. "I hope it's pizza, because I'm starved. Hope he makes it home before I get there," he joked.

"You are such an ass," Chloe laughed through her tears.

"Just relax, Sis, we'll find him soon." The call ended and Chloe felt completely alone again. She knew he was just trying to calm her fear, but he only called her Sis when he was concerned.

When Aaron arrived, Chloe was sitting on the edge of the couch, holding tight to her phone. "Not with Dad, then?" she said flatly, not looking up.

Saint Mary's Hospital

Alex was following the girl in grumpy silence, as she had shushed him and told him to walk softly past the doors to the 2nd floor. He noticed her steps made no sound, in fact, he wasn't sure she was actually touching the ground. They paused at the double doors to the third floor. She was watching him as if trying to decide something. Frowning slightly, she pushed open the doors and let them close behind her. Alex was stunned by her departure. Annoyed, he pushed through to follow. His mouth was open, ready with an admonishment, but then he paused at the sight before him. It was just a glance but as he focused, he could see a difference from the corner of his eye. Looking straight ahead, everything looked fine, empty and dark, but fine. Yet as he stared, he began to see through the illusion he was sure was emanating from the girl.

The picture changed before him. The hall slowly faded from an empty hospital corridor to an abandoned derelict. There was fallen tiles and peeling paint. Graffiti covered the walls and the front of the nurse's station. Whatever wasn't covered in foul language or filthy renditions of sexual anatomy was torn, broken, or shattered. "Is that really the way you want to see this?" The girl he had been following asked as she stepped into view.

Alex yelped, staggering back in spite of himself. She was emaciated to the point that she looked like a walking skeleton, and she was dressed in a filthy nightgown that someone had put a matted, disheveled black wig on. "I'm sorry, I'm sorry," he cried, turning from her, his eyes shut tight. Taking a steadying breath, he opened his eyes and allowed them to be fooled by the illusion again. His gaze returned to the girl. She appeared the way he had first seen her—but now, it was as if two pictures were dissolving into one another, and the hint of the gaunt girl stayed in his vision.

"Well now that *that* unpleasantness is out of the way…" She advanced purposefully toward him, her small hand outstretched. "We'll be safe here, for now. My name is Norah Sheppard, and you are?"

Alex hesitated, then took her small icy hand in his. "Alex, and where am I, and how the hell did I get here?"

His hand began to burn from cold as she continued to hold and inspect it. "You're not dead," she stated simply, confusion in her tone.

"No, I'm not."

"You are actually standing here. This is odd." She spoke as if she was inspecting a piece of furniture. "Not an astral projection, not a psychic manifestation—you are actually here?" She was circling him as she spoke. "What is your connection to this place?"

"I don't even know where this place is," Alex replied, trying to keep the annoyance out of his voice. "You, obviously, are dead, but you seem more substantial." Now he was starting to circle her. Like two predators ready to pounce at the first sign of weakness.

"You are not surprised or frightened that I am a ghost."

"No, but as I mentioned, there seems to be more to you than the usual specter or phantom," Alex replied as they continued to circle each other.

"The others think I put too much energy into maintaining these appearances, and to be able to touch and feel." Her voice was quiet and full of annoyance. "But I would rather not look at this place as it has become, or as I became."

"That makes perfect sense to me," he shrugged, "but it still does not explain how I got here or why." Alex and Norah halted their dance to stare at each other questioningly. "I think you are the first ghost I have met that controls her surroundings."

Her brow twitched inquisitively. "You have met a lot of ghosts?"

Laughing, Alex confirmed, "Dozens—hell I am even engaged to one." He hurried on to explain, as the look he was receiving seemed to doubt his honesty or sanity. He told her how he and Chloe had met at the Sterben House. How she had been killed and the circumstances of her death. How her spirit was meant to be a sacrifice, but she had lingered due to an unfulfilled contract with a demon. And how this led to her eventual return to corporeal form.

Norah frowned. "I guess being experimented on, tortured, abused, and left to die after being forced to watch your only friend in the world being murdered doesn't count for much in the resurrection world." Aghast, Alex reached out to her, but faltered. "You said 'the others?'"

"You didn't think it was just me, did you?"

"Well, sorta—I mean, you and that thing that was downstairs. Wait, that must be how I got here!" He slammed a fist into his hand, remembering, "Alistair!"

"Alistair?" She cocked her head to the side. "Is that the name of the new thing? It didn't feel human; well, not entirely. *You* felt human, but it has been so long since I met a live one." She frowned, "At least one that wasn't full of hormones, or dying from drink or drugs, so I didn't know." She frowned again, shaking her head. "I am not really making sense."

"No, I get it," Alex reassured her. "Alistair wants revenge on Chloe. He must have brought me here." Alex was pacing now. "But if he did, why were you the first person I met?" He was looking her over again.

"That is a fine question," Norah replied, stepping back from the scrutiny.

Realizing he was glowering down at her, he took a step back. "Sorry. Tell me about this place and if you can, what happened to you?"

"Well, I guess we should start with where you are. Welcome to Saint Mary's Hospital and Sanitarium," she exclaimed, holding her arms out wide.

1953

"Come on Billy, you promised." Norah poked Billy's shoulder repeatedly. "You said when it gets warmer, you would take me outside."

"Yeah, I know, but…" he shifted uncomfortably on the edge of her bed. She was sitting propped up by several pillows. She still looked incredibly small to him. "You know, I…" he faltered, causing her to laugh.

"You made that promise thinking I wouldn't live long enough to have to fulfill it." She flopped back into the pillows, laughing, earning her a few dirty looks from the other patients in the open ward. Billy's face reddened in guilt, causing her to laugh even more. "A promise is a promise." Norah sat up, all laughter gone. Billy could feel her blue eyes bore into the side of his face. He refused to meet her gaze.

"The doctors have said it is unhealthy for you to be out at night," Billy replied, without conviction. In the few months since her arrival, Billy had taken his assignment seriously. Dr. Pryor told him she was his responsibility. From the time she finally woke from the accident to find out her family was gone, he had been by her side. Since he already lived on the grounds, he had stayed with Norah through her nightmares. He was there when she came out of her treatments, sick and frail. He hated to refuse her anything. He was guilty of sneaking in sweets and special food from the burger stand down the road. He brought her books and magazines; anything he could to bring the rare smile to her face. He glanced at her as she lay back on the pillows, staring at the ceiling. His resolve shattered at her look of disappointment. He knew she was playing him, but he could do nothing to stop it.

"I thought you were my friend," she mumbled, and pulled a small stuffed wolf out from under her pillow. "I guess you are my only friend, Horo." The toy had received the name through a misunderstanding. He had presented it to her the first day she had woken after the accident. She had called Billy her hero, but through the pain and swelling, he thought she named the wolf. The name stuck, as did Billy's desire to live up to what she had called him.

"Knock it off, Norah," he grumbled. "Fine, fine—if you keep quiet, I will take you outside." Her squeal of joy was hushed by a panicky Billy. Taking Norah out of the ward at night would only feed into the whispers of the nurses and some of the other patients. He knew what they thought. He was only a couple of years older than she was. He shook the thought away. He turned to see her staring at him with that look on her face, like she knew exactly what he was thinking. He looked away, feeling his face burning again. "Give me an hour, then meet me at the usual place." He got up from her bed. Not looking at her, he whispered, "I am not waiting one minute longer. If you get caught—" he didn't say what would happen. He knew she was trying not to kick her feet in excitement.

An hour later, Billy checked his watch as he stood at the bottom of stairs, holding the handle of a wheelchair. He knew she would not be happy to see it, but this was his condition. If she wanted to go out into the moonlight, she was going to be in the chair. The thought of what had happened when she snuck out on her own not long after her arrival caused sweat to break out on his brow.

He had been walking across the grounds when he heard a whimper. The snow was falling and had already started to cover the small form lying next to a bench. He had lifted her effortlessly from the ground. He told himself it was panic that made him think he saw something odd about her. Her face had been distorted, less human—and her teeth! He shuddered and rechecked his watch. It was one minute past the rendezvous. Swearing under his breath, he took a step toward the doorway back into the hospital, then to the door that led outside before turning to the stairs. If she had been caught sneaking out… He swore again, deciding he had to make sure she was okay. As soon as his foot hit the first step, he heard her sigh.

"I wasn't sure you would come to find me." She smiled, stepping out from the shadows. She approached shyly. Billy sucked in a breath. She was not in her normal hospital gown. Her hair was brushed and lay nicely on her shoulders, and a pale yellow sweater covered those shoulders. She wore a light blue skirt the came to just above her knees. She smiled at him, then looked away quickly.

"You, you look," Billy swallowed nervously, "you look nice." He finished lamely, cursing himself.

"You think so?" Norah smiled at him. "Thanks." The smile slipped a little when she saw the chair. Her mouth opened, closed, opened again as she cocked her head to one side. But then she smiled at Billy and sat down, allowing him to push her through the door into the sweet-smelling spring night air. He took her to the same bench where he had found her months before.

"You know, I'm fine." She smiled as she sat next to him on the bench. He could feel the warmth of her leg as she moved close to him. He was aware of how small and delicate she looked. He smiled, knowing she was far stronger than she appeared. She had proven a formidable foe to both the boy and girl bullies in the ward, and even against several of the doctors and nurses. He remembered her holding off a doctor that annoyed her. She had used an IV stand in a disciplined manner that told of some kind of training. Laughing, he brought it up.

Norah explained it was a type of martial arts her father had taught her. Their family had learned many self-defense techniques over the centuries. "He always told me I had to learn this way, because the normal way had not passed to me." Her brow furrowed as she said it. "I never knew what he meant. I asked him when my sister stopped training with me, but he didn't explain." She stared off into the dark trees in the distance. "He started telling me something the night of the accident." She unconsciously balled her fists. Billy had seen her do this before. She wouldn't notice how tightly she was clenching until her fingernails had dug into her palms to the point that they were bleeding. "He said…" She glanced down as Billy unfurled her fists to hold her hands. Even though her grip was tight she squeezed his hands in thanks. "He said my blood was tainted. He said if we couldn't clean my blood it would kill me." She looked straight into his eyes. "Then something happened. Something happened to me and… and," tears formed then spilled down her cheeks. "I think I caused the accident."

Billy saw the moon reflecting in her fathomless black pupils. Her pupils continued to expand, pushing the blue, then the whites away. He leaned back, still holding her hands. Her mouth was open with her heavy breathing. Her upper canines showed long and sharp. Billy pulled back his hands in pain. Her nails had turned to claws that cut at his arms. Billy fell backward off the bench. Norah fell forward and he could only see her hands and lower legs. Then she was on all fours, whimpering. Scuttling away, he stopped to rub at his eyes. The tiny girl was growing before his eyes. Billy clamped his hands tight over his eyes as she cried out.

Something silver with a red tuft on the end stuck into the neck of the hairy beast that fell smashing the bench.

"Oh Billy, I really wish you had not seen that." Doctor Pryor sighed. He was holding an odd-looking gun in the crook of his elbow. A sharp pain sent stars into Billy's vision, then darkness followed.

Where and How

"Arthur is not stupid," Liza spoke, slightly annoyed, "he knows something is amiss." Aaron dismissed the thought with a wave.

Chloe looked at Liza pleadingly. "I don't want to bring Arthur into this."

"Yeah, that last fight with Alistair took a lot out of Pops." Aaron was pacing, waving his hand as he read an ancient book. Liza watched with ever-diminishing patience. "Must be something wrong with the translation, I'm not getting anything." He grunted, slamming the book shut.

Jumping up and swiping the book from his hands Liza glared at him. "There is nothing wrong with the translation." She shot him a look that caused him to take a step back. "There is however everything wrong with the discipline of the caster!"

She muttered something in Gaelic that Chloe decided was most likely unkind. Liza was now muttering in another tongue neither Aaron nor Chloe understood. Her movements became more fluid. Liza's body was almost snake-like in its swaying. Chloe opened her mouth to say something, but she was immediately hushed by Aaron. Liza was swaying and moving around the living room, her strange chanting increasing in volume. Chloe jumped as Liza stopped and grabbed her hand. Liza cupped Chloe's hand into a cylinder. Yanking Chloe forward, Liza blew through Chloe's empty hand, sending a shower of dust through the entire room.

The room disappeared for a moment. As the dust settled, Chloe gasped. The figure of Alex, made of dust, was sitting on the couch. He was looking at something they couldn't see. He slowly rose from the couch and took a step forward toward the end of the room. As he went, the room changed ahead of him, extending into the distance. "Where is that?" Chloe demanded. Aaron hushed her again. Dust Alex took another step forward, and his hand was stretched out. He took another step and disappeared into a hall with windows along one wall. Before the image vanished, Chloe saw the face of a young girl look into the living room. Then the image vanished, leaving them standing in Chloe's immaculately clean living room.

"What happened?" Chloe asked. "So no one took him, he just got up and walked through a, a..." She cast around for the right word to describe what had happened.

"A different dimension?" Aaron asked, looking to Liza for an explanation.

Liza moved forward toward the rear wall, her hands held out in front of her, feeling the air and the remnants of the disturbance. "It was a portal," she said softly. Turning her head as if she was listening to the wall, "but not to another dimension—it was our own." She took a step back, looking at the fireplace in concern. "Someone or something powerful was looking for something."

"Well, I'm glad it isn't specific; *that* would be too easy to deal with," Aaron grumbled in Chloe's ear. Liza glared at him. "Most likely they were looking for you, Chloe." Aaron offered.

Chloe stared at the wall, replaying what she had witnessed. "Maybe," she said, looking from the couch to the wall, "or they were looking for a bridge." Chloe sat where Alex had been, and a small smile crept across her face. "I can still feel him." She got up just as he had, except her eyes were closed, just like Liza's had been. Holding her hand out, she slowly approached the wall. "The girl," she whispered.

"Girl? What girl?" Aaron demanded, looking from Chloe to Liza.

Liza moved to stand next to Chloe, and her hand joined Chloe's. "It is help for her that is sought, but not her who called him?" Liza questioned.

Chloe frowned, "Someone is looking for help, but not necessarily for themselves. They are worried about her."

Liza's eyes flew open, as did Chloe's. They stared at each other for a second. Aaron looked from one to the other, and then they both turned to him and spoke as one. "Since he arrived."

"He? He who?" Aaron demanded, "Alex?"

"No, Alistair," Chloe replied through a grimace.

Baiting the Trap

Alistair marveled that the good doctor could light the moldy cigar without setting his desiccated hand on fire. "You see, I have always been interested in prolonging life." Dr. Pryor offered the box to Alistair, who politely refused. "It was when I was in the service that I finally found some very interesting information." He began to pace along a track in the carpet that had long since been worn through to the floorboards. "I understand there are things in the shadows, and those who know how to harness the powers of the universe." He saluted Alistair with the cigar. "I have come across many, shall we call them, *special people* in my research." Alistair glanced sideways at the doctor, who seemed to understand what he was thinking and waved it off with the cigar. Ash and crumbling tobacco fell to the floor as he did. "I have met with witches and wizards but could never equal their skills. Of course, I couldn't extricate the power from them either." He smiled at Alistair, and it made Alistair uncomfortable.

"Are you saying you experimented on my kind?" Alistair could not hide his surprise. He couldn't fathom how a mortal could have captured a practitioner of the arts.

"Yes, yes," he again waved off Alistair's concern, "that was in the early days. A simple thing really to bind your magic, not to worry. It is far easier to have you willingly cooperate; the spells last longer." He smiled. "What I have found is your use of magic does prolong your life, but there are those creatures who have magic *flowing through* them, so they do not need to use magic to stay young." He was standing behind his large oak desk now, his grey eyes staring at Alistair. "The thing about these beings, is they are far harder to trap, and when their effects begin to wane, well." He motioned to his body. "Since your kind know where to find these things, I figured you would be a great asset to me." He watched Alistair for a moment. "You, of course, are wondering what is in it for you?" The grin disappeared. "I let you keep your power."

Alistair's rage burned but he smiled at the walking corpse. "I would be more than happy to assist you." He shot a bolt of lightning straight above Dr. Pryor, who ducked behind the desk as the ceiling exploded. "But do not threaten me! I am not some low-level magician that could be bound. I felt your feeble attempt the second we crossed the threshold." Alistair stood, glaring down at the cowering doctor.

Smiling, Dr. Pryor stood up slowly. He began to clap but noticed the crushed and crumbling cigar. Throwing it away, he applauded Alistair and bowed. Next, he reached into the desk to pull out what looked like a gun. Alistair reacted quickly, and the room exploded in light as magic hit magic. Gloom returned.

Dr. Pryor said casually, "Got this little trinket from a witch; she was very powerful. This kept her safe from attack, so long as she had it with her. It is also quite useful as a weapon." He smiled at the instrument. "So, shall we discuss how to assist each other?" Warily the two began to discuss what would be gained and what was expected from an alliance.

"How would you feel about a ghost coming back from the dead after seventy years?" Alistair asked. Dr. Pryor answered by licking his lips hungrily. Suddenly his head snapped up.

"Someone is here."

Alistair smiled at his new friend. "I'll take care of them." He bowed as he left the room. This would be how he lured Chloe to him. Then he would let the good doctor take care of her. Alistair laughed to himself as he felt the air. Two mortals had just pulled up outside. His smile broadened. They had met ghosts before. He could feel it, and the desperation of one of the two to meet more. Alistair laughed as he felt the mood of the other person. This one couldn't have wanted anything less than to meet another specter.

Chance Encounter

Alex waited as Norah's arms fell to her sides. "Well, what can I say, it was a hospital." She shrugged, making her way to the broken window. The slight breeze that seeped in blew through her like a wind across water. She lightly tapped at the small crack in the lower corner of the glass. "Oh, the head doctor was so revered," she spat. "He had some arrangement with the Army and the government to take in people who couldn't pay." A cold trickle of air blew across her finger, and she watched the ripples move across her hand. "That is how I ended up here. After my family was killed." Norah paused. Movement down on the overgrown driveway caught her attention. Alex joined her to watch a van pull up. It stopped right at the bottom of the entry steps.

Alex swallowed a laugh as a woman wearing a black shawl and lace on her head stepped out of the passenger side. She adjusted her odd clothing while a thin man with graying hair exited the driver's side. Norah smiled as she watched the man stretch and frown at the woman's preening. Words were exchanged that Norah and Alex could not hear. The man threw his hands up in the air in frustration. He disappeared around to the back of the van. Alex and Norah glanced at each other, then back to the odd scene. Alex caught a glimpse of something Norah could not see. Whatever he saw caused a frown on his face.

She was about to ask when the man reappeared. He carried a long black box that fit onto his shoulder. His hand went to a smaller box attached to it that looked kind of like a camera lens. When the man put his eye to a tube coming from the body of the box, she was sure of it. "Oh great, ghost hunters," Alex muttered.

Norah's eyes went wide with fear. "People hunt us?" She gripped his arm tight. Alex was always amazed that an apparition could grip so hard.

"No, not hunt in that manner—hey, you're hurting me." Alex pried her hand gently from his arm. "Mostly they are people who shoot videos." He paused at the confusion on her face. "You know, um, live TV."

"I heard about those." She nodded, brow still furrowed. "I never saw one. They had them here, after," her eyes stared into the past, "by the time I escaped this place was already closed." She turned again to face him. Alex stumbled on what to say. He wanted to ask about the escape, but she interrupted again. "So, they make TV shows about hunting ghosts, but they don't hunt them?" She turned her attention back to the window. The woman was making weird exaggerated gestures to the hospital façade. When she turned around, Norah suppressed a laugh at the blatant disdain the cameraman had for his subject. A smile shot back onto the man's face and the lady turned back to face him.

Alex snorted at their actions. "You see the weird lady dressed like a Halloween gypsy?" She nodded, a smirk playing at the corner of her mouth. "She'll be standing in one of the rooms here later. It will be dark, and she'll be explaining all the rumors of whatever: murder, death, rampant disease, whatever." Alex shrugged. "Well, they will be in the dark, calling on the spirits. Nothing ever happens; they claim to hear things and basically just scare themselves. Then they try to show a shadow as a demon or some sound. They tell you what to listen for, then play it so you think that you hear it too."

"This seems to bother you quite a bit," Norah said turning from the window.

"As I said, I am engaged to someone who used to be dead." For the first time ever, Alex felt a little embarrassed by it. Not because Chloe had been a ghost, but because he was telling a ghost. Knowing what happened with Chloe was not likely to happen to her made him uncomfortable. Shaking it off, he said, "She can still easily interact with, um, the deceased. We have dealt with these fools before. More than once we have been across the room with the actual ghost, while the hunters swore they were being touched and talked to." A wry smiled light up his face. "This one time, the ghost actually laughed. She scared them so bad they ran out of the house." Norah laughed along with him as she glanced out the window.

Suddenly her excitement grew as they watched the pair disappear under the covered stairs. "Oh, no-no-no. They really shouldn't be here. Not while your Alistair and our doctor are here," she exclaimed, grabbing a small stuffed wolf from the windowsill that Alex had not noticed there before. "Just in case," she muttered as she brushed past him, then turned and grabbed his arm again. "They're coming in. Let's go warn them before it's too late." The sound of their running feet caused several pale and transparent faces to poke out of rooms as they, or mostly Alex, thundered down the hall. The door at the top of the stairs swung shut and Norah stopped Alex. Rubbing his chin, Alex's eyes demanded an explanation. "You are alive. If they see you, what will happen?" Alex stared at her, his mind trying to catch up to her question. Several faces appeared through the door. Norah waved them away, as Alex ignored their stares.

"I don't know, I mean, what?"

"Will they believe this place is haunted if you are here? Will that scare them away?" She rubbed her chin as she thought about it. "Or will seeing someone alive make them think this is a hoax and then they'll leave?" She mumbled more to herself than to him, "Damn it, come on, let's see if they are easily frightened." At a loss, Alex shrugged to her back and followed the young ghost down the dark stairwell.

Alex tried to keep track of the lefts and rights, as it felt like he was being dragged through a labyrinth. Finally, holding a finger to her lips, she paused. As quietly as possible, she eased open the last door to the balcony overlooking the lobby. Silently Norah passed through. She could hear the woman speaking in a loud whisper.

"Saint Mary's Sanatorium was once the pinnacle of care for long-term patients." The woman spread her arms wide, turning slowly on the spot as she continued to explain. "Now it is a shell, housing drug users and thugs." Her arms dropped to her sides. "Did you get that?" The cameraman did not respond. "Mike! Did you get that?" she demanded, the ethereal whisper gone from her sharp voice. Norah frowned at the change. Moving cautiously to not be seen, she looked out of the broken dirty window. She could now see the words painted across the side of the van. *Linda Blackstone, Haunting Investigator.* Norah laughed once, immediately covering her mouth. "Mike, I am talking to you." Linda stamped her foot. Mike was looking up at the balcony. "Michael Krewleski, what am I paying you for?"

"To follow you around while you scare yourself in abandoned buildings," Mike replied in a bored tone, deciding he hadn't actually heard anything.

"You were there at Sterben. You saw it too," she shouted. "You want to confirm what we saw just as much as I do."

"Yeah, maybe, or maybe it *was* just some teenager playing a prank."

"That was no prank," her voice dropped back to its staged whisper, "the spirits want to commune with me." She stared at him. "That was good—you should have been rolling."

"I don't tell you how to find creaking rooms or scare kids having sex. So you don't tell me how to shoot this crap."

"This crap pays us pretty damn good," she growled. "Okay." She rolled her head on her shoulders, took a deep breath and waited. Mike put the camera up to his eye and she began again. "This once beautiful place of healing was abandoned in the early two thousands—"

"Oh crap, not her," Alex groaned as he crouched next to Norah. "Her name is Linda Blackstone," he rolled his eyes at the name. "It's probably actually Smith or something."

"She investigates hauntings?" Norah whispered, suppressing a giggle. She was peeking over the safety railing on the short wall. Ducking quickly, she again covered her mouth as she laughed. "I think Mike the cameraman heard me." She was having a hard time covering her mirth.

"Be careful," Alex warned, but couldn't help smiling. Norah slowly rose to look between the rail and the wall. Down below Linda was making quite the production of swooping along the old moldy reception desk.

"It was then that the horrible truth came out," Linda explained in a dramatic stage whisper. "Okay, let's move to one of the wards." She spun on her heel, a happy bounce in her step. Mike let the camera fall from his shoulder and rest on his arm. He shook his head at Linda then glanced back to the balcony.

"Should we try to scare them?" Norah asked, "Please?" She looked disgusted. Alex raised an eyebrow. She huffed, "It's like watching the drama club in high school." She frowned. "So over-dramatic and full of..." Her pale cheeks changed slightly. Alex realized she was blushing. "Well, you get the idea." She wasn't looking at Alex now.

"WWOOOOooooooooGGGGGGGGGGGGGGGG" Alex cupped his hands to his mouth, howling like a wolf. Norah's eyes widened as the camera fell to the floor, followed by Linda tripping backward over an old torn cushion. Norah was biting her index finger to keep from laughing. Tears ran down her face and her body shook with laughter. "NOOOOTTTHHHHINGGG heeeerrrreeee buuut dooooooOOOOOOOOOOMMMMM." Alex called, although the effect was marred with his suppressed laugh at the end. Norah could not hold back. The lobby echoed with peals of their laughter.

"HAHA, very funny," Linda yelled. "We have permission to be here. One call and the police will be here in five minutes." Linda was holding a small black box that lit up on one side as she held it. "I suggest you shut up and get lost!" Keeping low, Norah pulled Alex along toward the doors. Both stumbled as they continued to laugh.

Recovering themselves, their smiles slowly slid off. "This isn't good. They think we are messing with them." Alex frowned.

"I guess you shouldn't have laughed. It is a bit less frightening that way." She stared at him, her hand on her hips in a manner reminiscent of Chloe. The thought of her made his heart ache. Her face softened at the look of pain in his eyes. "Look, maybe this is a good thing. They believe in ghosts, so maybe they will believe you were transported here, and help you get home."

"I don't know, they may just call the police." He thought for a second, "that would be one way to get out. I could call Chloe and come back to help you."

"Why would you come back?" Norah asked, stunned.

"Because you shouldn't be stuck here either, and Alistair is kind of…" it was his turn now not to meet her gaze, "our problem, not yours."

She placed a hand on his forearm. "That is sweet. Stupid, but sweet." Norah turned from him. It took Alex a moment to register she had stopped to wait for him. "Come on," she motioned for him to follow. Alex was about to argue, but decided he was going to help one way or another. As they hurried down the last set of stairs to the double doors leading to the lobby, Norah spoke again. "I know what you are thinking." She paused at the door, hand on the faded paint. "You are going to help this silly little girl even though she is telling you to stay out of it." Alex began to protest. "If you think you can help, then I welcome it. The thing is, you don't know what you are up against." She turned to push through the doors.

Alex caught her by the arm. His ability to grab her was a shock. "Maybe so, but you have no idea who my friends are." She stared at him expectantly. Her gaze again flustered him. "I well, there is Chloe and Liza, um she is like a 900-year-old witch, and my brother, who she is teaching to be a witch." He realized he was sounding rather lame, and the raised eyebrow of Norah did nothing for his confidence. They stood staring at each other until Norah let out a bark of a laugh.

Pushing the door open, she shook her head. "Witches, really." The creak of the door mixed with her laugh caused both Mike and Linda to look around wildly for the source.

"Uh, yeah, okay," Mike swallowed, "that was creepy. You didn't tell me this was a children's hospital," he yelled, pointing. Norah was partially visible as she pushed through the door. Her laugh at Alex echoed loudly across the open space. "Linda, this isn't cool," Mike shouted, taking a step back.

Linda's face retained its annoyed frown. She had not seen what he had. She was still trying to figure out the source of the laughter. "Oh, grow a pair. It's just some damn kids messing around. There were no children here. This place was a hospital. They got a contract to care for vets who had been wounded. Then as things changed this became more of a nursing home."

"Is that when they started letting people die?" Mike asked, still looking over his shoulder. A door slammed to their right, causing Mike to smack his face into the camera as he tried to catch what had gone through it. Linda glared at him.

"You can't film it if you don't use the camera." She followed with an angry mutter, "Moron." Norah had heard the exchange. She decided she liked Mike but not Linda. Alex pulled her back through the door.

"Wait, something is not right," Alex whispered. A shiver ran through Norah as well. They both glanced down the hall they were in. Windows sat at constant intervals. All they had to do was get to the end. An old gurney sat neglected along the wall. It was covered in empty bottles and fallen plaster. As Alex approached, something distracted him. Norah reached out, but too late. Alex tripped over a fallen ceiling tile, sending the gurney's contents smashing to the floor. Norah swore, pushing Alex toward the exit. Seconds later, Linda smashed through the door. She searched the hall for a split second before her eyes landed on Norah, standing clear as day in the shadows. Mike appeared over Linda's shoulder, the camera on his shoulder, where a little red light was blinking.

"Alright, little missy," Linda boomed, "we'll see how you like meeting the police." Linda pushed a button on the black rectangle she carried. The face of it lit up with little pictures.

Norah contemplated the device for a moment before laughing and running down the hall. The phone fell from Linda's hand. In the shadows Norah appeared to be a solid girl, yet when she passed through the sunlight of the windows she disappeared, re-appearing in the next shadow. At first, it was only her laugh that filled the hallway as she ran.

"Wait, little girl, wait!" Linda called, scooping up her phone and giving chase. Mike stood stunned for a moment, watching the girl appear and disappear down the hall. The sight of Linda's trailing shawls brought him back to himself, and the news videographer he had been took over. Keeping the whole scene in the frame as he ran, the video would have been fantastic—if only his equipment were just a bit better.

Norah disappeared through the double doors at the end of the hall. Alex was waiting for her. "Come on, they are not the scaring type. You have to lure them out," she called, pulling him after her into the same examination room they had hidden in before. "Get behind me. I think I can make the darkness impervious.

The tension built and Alex held his breath. "Wait, why are we hiding?" Alex stood up, breathing normally. The tension began to wane as they continued to be alone on the other side of the doors.

"Good question." Norah relaxed. Alex noticed the darkness seemed to become thinner. He also noticed that a growling sound that had accompanied them from the time they hit the shadows now seemed to be fading. Before he could question it, Norah demanded, "What is keeping them?" She stepped into the hall. "This could be really bad." Norah wore her concern across her small porcelain face.

"I have no idea," Alex commented, taking Norah by her hand. "I bet they got scared when they saw you run down the hall." He spoke casually, but a billion creatures stirred in his stomach. "Come on, let's see what they are up to." Reaching the doors, Alex took a deep breath, smiled at Norah, then carefully eased the doors open. Norah gasped at the sight.

Linda lay face down in the middle of the moldy carpeted hall. Mike stood stock still, the camera still on his shoulder, the little red light blinking. Standing in front of them, with his back to Alex and Norah, stood a man. At least Norah thought it was a man. It had a man's voice, but there was something else in that voice, malice she had never heard the like of before. As they watched, a new carpet stain was beginning to form around Linda.

"Listen very carefully," the man rasped. "In this place are the souls of twelve people." He sniffed the air, "One of whom is a young girl, about the age you were when you died." He raised his arms; the tattered cloak he wore was filthy. "You will, of course, want to help—"

"Is he talking about me?" Norah whispered to Alex. He did not answer. There was a look on his face she had not seen before. His eyes held a fierceness that scared her. His mind seemed to be taking in his surroundings, making plans. He nodded once as he seemed to come to a conclusion.

"Yes, and I am sure this message is for Chloe," Alex growled. Norah didn't feel like he was talking to her. "If this goes the way I think it is going, we will need a place to hide out."

Norah hesitated. "Back upstairs in the ward. But if something bad happens, go to the morgue." Her eyes told him of her fear. "It is okay, I know someone there." She tried to act calm. "He's a bit odd; lives in drawer five. T… t… tell him you are my friend, and he will protect you." Alex already knew this was the last place on earth she wanted to go. "If all else fails and we get separated," she steeled her nerves, "We meet in the morgue, okay?"

"Okay," he said, but doubt crossed his face. "Why would we get separated? I would prefer to stay with you. You know your way around here."

"I can pass through walls, and you can't."

"Right." Looking back through the door, Alex's anger grew. "Alistair," he breathed, listening to the wizard pontificate, his words full of threats and malice. Norah was about to say something when Alex pointed. "Shhh, we need to hear this."

"So, I have explained what I can do to these souls if you do not come to face me." Slowly Alistair began to rise into the air. The camera on Mike's shoulder began to shake, but he followed the ascension. Looking down, Alistair's finger shot toward the camera with menace. Mike jumped back, but recovered immediately, "I, Alistair Fox, promise this. You interfered in my plans. If you are the good Samaritan that you pretend to be, you will come to face me. Face me, and I will release them." In his other hand, Alistair produced a fog. In this fog, Norah saw the faces of many of the dead she knew. Only Alex's firm grip kept her from attacking the evil wizard. "Do nothing, and I will destroy them one by one. You have two days. I am firm on that point—every day that you dawdle, I will burn a soul." Flames shot through the fog in his hand.

Alistair was descending as Alex pulled Norah back from the door. Through the crack they could hear him speaking again. "You will make sure that video makes it to Chloe Miller, and I suggest you do it quickly." Mike let the camera drop from his shoulder, looked down at Linda's motionless body for a second, then ran for the lobby.

"This is not good at all," Alex hissed. Suddenly he felt a wave of icy air cascade over him. His vision blurred as his body went weightless, then in an instant his weight crashed down and he hit the floor. His head spun and his stomach protested. He was back in the ward. Norah sat even more pale and transparent next to Alex. She was leaning against a bed.

Norah tried to call out. Her voice failed her. Alex tried to move. He ended up on his side, wishing the world would stop spinning. Finally, Norah squeaked, "Everyone hide, we have an intruder and they are not here to help!" She turned back to Alex, and the strain of her warning had left tears gathered in her eyes. "We have to move." She tried to get up. She half raised herself before collapsing back down.

"Norah, please." Alex tried to crawl to her. "Where can we go?" He stumbled to a crouched position. Reaching out to her, he was silently glad she was ethereal, as he could barely lift himself. Norah draped an arm over his shoulder, then pulled the battered stuffed wolf from her gown.

"You said you would always be with me. You said we would stay together forever," she said, and hugged the battered stuffed wolf to her chest. Alex continued to pull her toward the hall.

"Norah, where can we hide?" Alex asked as ghosts flew in different directions around them.

She seemed to realize Alex was there. Weakly, she smiled at him, then at the wolf. "I know a place that will be safe." She stood a little straighter and began to help Alex move. "It's this way." She steered him along the hall to a door marked Staff Only. "It is only for a little while," she whispered to the wolf, "I promise." Alex thought it was just his mind due to whatever Norah had done to teleport them, but he swore the wolf toy moved.

"It's weird," Norah said as they traveled down a long narrow hall. "He didn't mention the others in the basement, or you."

"I'm warded against him finding me." Alex coughed. "Who is in the basement?" He didn't have time to dwell. The world was spinning, and he began to watch the black tunnels at the edge of his vision coming to a point. He was going to pass out and there was nothing he could do to stop it. "Uh, Norah, I think I might—."

1953

Billy woke slowly. His head was pounding and his vision blurred. He reached to check his head, but his arm wouldn't move. He tried the other hand. The fog in his mind was lifting fast. Billy realized he was strapped to a gurney. His arms and feet were bound in tight leather bindings. Fighting against the restraints, he wildly took in his surroundings. It was a smaller room, tiled with greenish-blue porcelain. A large examination light hung above him, glowing dimly. Turning his head, he could see a large mirror set about halfway up the wall. On the floor he could barely make out the holes in the cover of the drain. Just out of reach was a tray covered in a crisp white sheet.

"Let me out!" His voice betrayed the terror in his heart. "I am not a patient!" he screamed. "Dr. Pryor knows me, ask Dr. Pryor!" The light above him intensified, hurting his eyes. Stretching his neck, he could see a door open near his feet. "Ask Dr. Pryor! He knows me!" Struggling against his restraints, he tried to see the visitor's face. Slowly someone stepped into the pool of light. Billy stopped struggling. Letting his head flop onto the mattress, he let out an exhausted breath. "Dr. Pryor, I think there has been a mistake. Please let me up," Billy begged.

"Oh Billy, I wish that was the case." Dr. Pryor's soft voice sounded from somewhere above his head. The white cloth was whipped away, revealing gleaming steel implements. "I thought I could trust you, Billy." Dr. Pryor's face appeared upside down over Billy's. "When I made you her guardian, I thought I made it clear you were to take care of her."

"Norah, where is she?" Billy strained against the restraints. "She's in trouble. Something terrible was happening to her; we need to find her!" He struggled, as the memories of the night exploded into his mind. "Please Doctor, I need to find her." Thrashing about, he felt Dr. Pryor's cold strong hand press down on his head, forcing him to remain still.

"You were supposed to keep Norah in her ward." Billy's eye caught sight of a needle. A drop of red liquid fell from the tip. Then a sting in his arm told him he had been injected. "If you had done as you were told, none of this would be happening." Billy's back arched in agony. It felt like his blood was on fire. "You see…," Dr. Pryor's voice was calm and even as he took up a scalpel. Through the burning, Billy still felt the blade cut into his arm. He screamed. "I'm sorry, I can't understand you. It is very important you be able to communicate what you are feeling."

Tears were streaming from Billy's eyes. Through the watery blur, he could see the doctor examining a bloody piece of flesh. He knew it was from his body. The burning of his blood had slowed to a simmer. Taking in several deep lungfuls of air, he tried to calm down. Fighting the agony, he tried to speak. Dr. Pryor bent low to hear what he was attempting to say. "Norah," Billy gasped, and swallowing, he tried again. "Norah, where is she?" he shouted.

Dr. Pryor jumped back, rubbing his ear. "That was rude." Dr. Pryor commented, still rubbing his ear. "She is as well as can be expected, after what you let happen." Pain shot through Billy's arm again. Dr. Pryor looked at the chunk of the flesh, and a troubled look crossed his face. There was a clatter of metal on metal. It drowned out Billy's demand to know more about Norah. Suddenly one of the wounds in his arm was on fire. "Oh, that is much better." The burning was so intense Billy could only scream. Sweat and tears soaked the mattress under Billy's head. Dr. Pryor's face appeared over him again. "You should really thank her." Billy felt the blade slice into his arm at the same place the burning had just died down from. "Without her blood, none of these wounds would heal." Light flashed in the reflection of a bone saw. "Let's try something a bit more extensive."

After an eternity of pain and burning blood, Billy woke to a strong hand slapping his face. "I think we'll leave it there for today." As if Billy would find it funny, Dr. Pryor held up an empty syringe, "We may have to wait a day or two to continue." He looked disappointed. "Norah is such a small thing. If I take too much she might not survive." Billy could do nothing but cry silently in his pain and for Norah.

Time lost meaning in his greenish-blue hell. Billy lay naked, strapped to the gurney, as Dr. Pryor administered pain. He wanted to see the effects on Billy's damaged leg. He wanted to see how it affected hair growth by scalping Billy. Billy could never see his own body, but he knew he wouldn't recognize it. He became numb to the stabbing, slicing, and reconstructing. He would watch as his blood disappeared through the drain in the floor. All Billy could think of was Norah and what she must be going through. After a week, or maybe a month of the experiments, Billy had a realization. He felt his teeth and knew his tongue had finally grown back. He also realized he could move his arm. Pulling it free, he screamed at the sight. His hand was missing. At the end of his arm, small bones showed where his hand had started to grow back. Fighting his terror, he began trying to undo the strap on his still-whole hand.

Bits of bone splintered off as he worked the buckle. Finally, he was free. Blood covered his hand, making it slick as he tried to undo his leg bindings. His wrist stump was also bleeding freely through the holes left by the broken bones. Swinging his legs over the side of the gurney, his stomach would have emptied if it had anything in it to begin with. Long strips of flesh and muscle fell away as gravity took them. Putting weight on the leg brought the world spinning to the floor as the bone, not held by muscle or tendon, tore free. Dragging himself across the floor, he could hear muffled screams, *Norah*, he thought. Fighting and dragging himself inch by inch, he approached the door. Blood dripped from his hand as he reached out. Inches to the knob. He could make it. Looking back, he saw a thick path of blood showing his route. He would have to do something about that, or he would be too easy to find. He would find something to wrap himself in, get a crutch, find Norah, and get them out.

Slick bloody fingers had barely teased the doorknob when it flew open, knocking Billy backward. Through the lightning and exploding stars of pain, he could see the front wheels of a wheelchair. Hands and feet bound tight, her mouth gagged, was Norah. Her tears, muffled cry, and struggle to reach him tore at his heart.

"That was quite naughty, Billy," Doctor Pryor stepped around the oddly shaped orderly who was pushing the chair. Billy found he was wrong when he thought he had seen all the horrors the world could hold. This thing was not human and not quite animal. It looked like several beasts sewn together. It pushed Norah in front of the mirror, facing Billy. Another beast-man creature entered the room, and there was a familiar limp to the way it carried itself. It quickly removed the gore-encrusted gurney Billy had been living on. Moments later a beast-woman entered the room, pushing another chair. With the help of Norah's creature, she lifted Billy into the chair, strapping him in tight. "I think I will let you two get re-acquainted. Miss Norah may have a secret to tell you." The limping beast-man's eyes meet Billy's. The look they gave was one of deepest sympathy. "Come, we are leaving them alone." Dr. Pryor spoke calmly, but there was no mistaking the order. The beast-man hesitated, turned, then turned back to Billy. "I said come along," Dr. Pryor's voice held a dangerous note. The beast-man quickly pulled a towel from his coat to cover Billy's lap. He then hurried out the door. It was the first time Billy had ever seen the look of fury and hatred in Dr. Pryor's eyes.

"Billy, I am so sorry," Norah wept from across the room. Her gag sat around her neck like a collar.

Billy tried to smile. "As long as you are okay, I'm fine." His voice was gravely after not being used for anything but screaming for so long. He was relieved to see she did not seem to have suffered the same mutilations he had. Looking over his body for the first time, he could only describe it as a roadmap of pain.

"This is all my fault! If I hadn't made you take me out that night," Norah fought out through her tears, "he wouldn't have found out. He wouldn't be doing this to you."

"Norah, shh, shh, I'm fine." Billy lied. He frowned at his femur laying on the floor, barely attached to his ankle. "I had a little accident that is all. The doctor has been trying to help me." He was lying. He didn't want her to worry.

Anger flew over her face. "He's been making me watch," she screamed.

Preparations

Mike sat behind the steering wheel of the van, shaking uncontrollably. He was stuttering into his phone, his shaking hand rubbing over his face as he tried again to make the police understand. "No, Linda is dead!" he shouted into the phone. "The guy just appeared out of nowhere. Yes, I am up at Saint Mary's." Pulling the phone from his ear he stared at the face of it. "No!" he shouted, "I am not high. This guy just appeared, he threw lightning at her, then he floated up in the air…" Mike heard himself and hit the *end call* button. His rambling made it sound like he had killed her. Not daring to, but unable not to, he glanced up at the building. A dark veil seemed to be slowly dropping over the hospital. He glanced up at a window to see two faces staring down at him. A young woman turned away, while a man was shooing him away. He was mouthing *Go* and *Run*.

"Screw this!" Mike shouted, firing up the engine and putting the van into reverse. He saw the backup camera come on. A shout died in his throat when he saw that Alistair stood behind him. Mike turned around to face forward, trying to catch his breath. A knock on his window caused him to scream. The angry face of Alistair glared at him.

"Go find Chloe Miller!" Alistair commanded. "Not just the souls here are depending on you. Your own soul will burn if you don't hurry." Flames shot up around Mike. He was still screaming, completely unharmed, several minutes later. Finally regaining his composure, he smashed the accelerator, fleeing through the broken gate at the end of the driveway. He was sweating and crying in fear.

An hour later found Mike sitting on the side of the road. His finger hovered over a name in his contact list. *This is crazy*, his mind kept repeating. The phone was dialing, ringing, then a voice on the other end questioned Mike's name. Ten minutes later, Mike was driving again. The address his old friend at the police department had given him was punched into the vehicles GPS. His stomach tightened further. There was something about that name that haunted him.

***

Liza was intently searching through a huge ancient tome. Oliver the ghost cat wound through her ankles like smoke. Aaron had given up trying to decipher the obscure text and was scrolling through web pages. Liza's fist slammed into the book, sending dust flying. "Why is this so difficult?" she shouted. Aaron looked up, saw the scowl on her face, and disappeared behind the screen of his laptop.

Chloe appeared out of her bedroom, rubbing her eyes, with an ashamed grim look on her face. "Liza, I'm so, so sorry," she yawned, running her fingers through her hair to tame it. "I didn't sleep, and just now…" She swallowed a sob.

Liza's expression softened. "Oh, my bonnie lass. I didna' mean to wake you." Liza was on her feet, pulling Chloe into a hug. Aaron peeked from behind the screen. He loved it when she slipped into her brogue. The sight of Chloe brought the seriousness of the situation crashing back down on him. Chloe yawned again, waving her hand in front of her as if to fan the tiredness away. "We've been searching for ways to locate Alex," Liza explained, holding Chloe at arm's length. "You look dreadful; you need a cuppa." Liza busied herself in the kitchen.

"I'm sorry," Chloe apologized again, heading into the kitchen to get the tea Liza held out to her. "I was dreaming. I saw Alex." She sipped the steaming beverage. Liza was watching Chloe closely. Aaron was glancing to her nervously. "He is safe for the moment." Chloe continued. "I tried to talk to him, but he couldn't hear me." Chloe frowned but it was more of a confused frown than sad. "He was with a young girl." The frown deepened, "I get the feeling she could hear me. I'm positive she was a ghost."

"Well, you know, he does have a thing for dead girls," Aaron commented before he could stop himself.

Liza glared at him, but Chloe responded with a bored, "Ha ha." She took a sip of tea and closed her eyes, recalling more details. "No, wait." She concentrated on the girl's face, replaying the dream over and over in her mind.

"I could see Alex, and he was unconscious, but I could feel he was safe." Her head cocked to the side. "She was staring at me. She was saying something."

Chloe had been standing in a darkened cold room. Alex lay on some moldy blankets with a young girl crouched next to him. She nodded, then stood to face Chloe.

"Hello," Chloe nervously greeted the small ghost. "I'm Chloe. Is Alex okay?"

The ghost girl watched Chloe with interest. "You two are very odd," she replied. Chloe fought the urge to scream at the girl. "My name is Norah. I think he will be okay." She explained, turning her back to Chloe, "I had to get him to safety and the only way I could do that was to take him through with me." Chloe understood what Norah had done.

"Thank you," As Chloe, spoke the room around them began to blur.

Norah turned to say something to Chloe. Her eyes flew open. Reaching out to Chloe, she shouted, "Saint!"

Chloe felt a pull at the back of her skull, as if her head was about to explode. Then she was falling through darkness. She was aware she was being held up, picked up, and laid on the couch. Opening an eye a crack, she could see Aaron's pale worried face and hear Liza chanting a healing spell.

Fear the cat and Oliver were nudging her hand and foot. Seeing her stir, Liza stopped chanting. Her face, a mask of worry, turned to one of anger. "Don't do that again!" She paced back and forth. "Astral projection is not something to mess with." She threw her hands up in frustration. In an instant, she was pulling Chloe up into a hug. "Are you okay? What happened?"

"Did you see my brother? Is he really okay? Where is he?" Aaron demanded. He saw that she was calmer than before, so he pushed, "Is the other girl hotter than you?" He jumped back to avoid the slap he richly deserved from Chloe, but not in time to avoid the one to the back of the head from Liza.

"Ha-ha, dork," Chloe said with a groan as Liza helped her sit up. Aaron disappeared down the hall. When he returned, he handed Chloe several aspirin. "Thanks." Liza handed her some tea. "Damn it. She was about to tell me where they were, but I got pulled back." She tried to get up, wobbled, and sat back down. Aaron's arms stretched out, ready to grab her. "I'm okay, just need to rest for a moment." She saw his worry. "Really, I'm okay, and so is Alex." She let her head fall back against the pillows on the back of the couch. Her eyes closed against the light to see the vision of Alex laying on the floor, still tattooed to the inside of her eyelids. "I just wish I knew where." She groaned, pushing her balled fists against her eyes.

The chiming of the doorbell caused all three to look toward the door, even though from their angle they could not see it. "Who the hell could that be?" Aaron growled, making his way to the hall. Chloe didn't move from the couch. She was still trying to picture where she had seen Alex. A commotion at the door brought her to her feet. Liza was already moving quickly toward the raised voices.

"And just who the hell are you?" Aaron demanded. Liza was behind him, glowering at the man who stood stooped on the front porch.

"Who is it?" Chloe asked, trying to keep her growing migraine at bay.

"This guy says he needs to see you. Says he has a message for you, but he won't explain who it's from," Aaron called over his shoulder. Chloe sighed at their backs. She knew they were being protective, but she felt annoyed by it. She was not some shrinking violet, and if it was about Alex she wanted to know.

Turning the corner, Chloe recognized the man. It took her a moment to place the face. The man still wasn't looking up. He was just mumbling about being sent and only being the messenger.

"It is all right," Chloe stated, trying to push her way past her two friends. "What do you need to tell me?"

Nervously the man looked up at her. He was unshaven, and his eyes held apprehension and fear. "Chloe Miller?" he demanded. Grabbing Chloe by the shoulders, he shouted, "Are you Chloe Miller?"

"I suggest ye compose yourself, ya daft lunatic. I am not one to be trifled with," Liza exclaimed, pushing the man away. "Who are ye?"

"My name is Mike, but that doesn't matter." Mike shook his head and his arm shot out to grab Chloe again. Knowing that would be an extremely bad thing, Chloe pushed her way past Liza.

"I am Chloe Miller. What can I do for you?" She held up a hand to try to calm Liza. She could feel the crackle of energy coming from the witch's hands. Mike didn't seem to notice the danger he was in. His attention was completely on Chloe. Slowly a look of recognition crossed Mike's face.

You're her." It wasn't a question; his eyes flew wide. "I… you, you, the girl in the house, how are you here?" He took a step back and shook his head. He jammed his hand into a pocket and shouted, "Here," thrusting a DVD into her hands. "I am done with this. I did what I was told." He backed away. "I don't want any more part in this," he yelled. Before anyone could ask anything, he was running to his van. Chloe took a step out onto the porch. Mike saw her pursuit. She could see the panic on Mike's face as he threw the van into reverse. The tires screeched as the van whipped out of the driveway. Before she could take another step, rubber screamed and smoked as he sped off.

"What the bloody hell was that all about?" Liza demanded of the fading taillights.

Trapped

It took Alex several tries before he was able to push sleep away. At first, he had no idea where he was, but as the fog lifted, he remembered the hospital. Now he had no idea where in the hospital he was because it was pitch black. Sitting up, he reeled from the musty smell. He could smell it on his hands, clothes, and even his hair. Getting up, he realized he was still quite weak and very hungry. Feeling his way around in the dark sent him stumbling over the random detritus in the room. Some things clanged against the floor while others squished unpleasantly.

Coming to the end of the third wall, he thought, don't tell me I was already beside the door when I woke up! Halfway along the final wall, he felt the outline of the door frame. And moving past the door, his foot hit the soft bedding he had awoken on. Typical. Still unable to see anything, he found the doorknob. It moved under his hand.

Throwing himself flat against the wall, he hoped the door would swing in and hide him. Swearing loudly in his mind, he saw the pale light spill in from the hall. Norah poked her head in. "Seriously, that was where you were going to hide?" Alex could see he was in a very small room, or more like a large closet. The floor was scattered with old buckets, chamber pots, and soaked ceiling tiles and towels. Water continued to drip onto them from a dirty hole in the ceiling. "Come on, we need to get you out of here."

Following her to the hall, he noticed she seemed to have recovered a little as well. "Thank you for helping me," Alex said.

Norah turned to face him. Her face held curiosity. "What else could I do?"

"You could have left me," Alex replied, a little shocked at her question.

"Would you have preferred that?" She stopped and studied his face. All he could do was stare down at her. His mouth opened and closed a few times as he tried to answer. Finally, he found the words. "No?" He spoke, unsure now what he was answering.

"Ok, next the time you are possibly going to be killed, I'll wait until you ask for help," Norah replied, obviously annoyed.

"Um, no, that is okay. Thank you," he finished uncertainly. Norah dropped her hands from her hips, turned and continued to lead him down the hall. "She's like Chloe's evil little sister," he grumbled.

"That's not nice," Norah called from a door with an exit sign above it.

"It is so quiet now," Alex said, trying to change the subject. "Where are the others?" Now it was his turn to look annoyed. "There were several others here before." She shrugged as she disappeared through the door. His jaw clenched as he pushed the door open and followed her faint glow down the dark stairs. "Hey, where did they go? Are they safe?"

"Right now, they are safe." She stopped so suddenly that Alex stepped into her. Jumping back, he failed to suppress the shiver. Norah ignored the encroachment. "What would happen if I told you where they were, and you got caught before we could get you out?" she demanded. The fire in her eyes told him she expected an honest answer.

"Alistair would torture me until I told him where they were," he replied quietly.

"And?" she demanded.

"And if I don't know where they are, I can't tell him." He felt like he had been scolded. "Wait a minute—how old were you when...." He suddenly felt awful for even asking.

"A few months shy of eighteen." She shrugged.

"Well, then, that um, makes me the adult, so you need to listen to me." Alex tried to sound mature. She turned around to look up at him. He rolled his shoulders and stood up straight. She was tiny, so he had about a good foot or more on her in height. She blinked at him expectantly. "Right. You need to get us out of here so I can contact my friends." He stated this with authority. He became uncomfortable under her gaze. Finally, he couldn't think of why she was just staring. "Well, lead the way."

Norah curtsied, and then pushed open the door next to them. Alex immediately knew something was wrong. Norah rolled her eyes and stepped toward the opening.

Alex pulled her back. Wrenching her arm free, she glared at him. "I can't smell the outside; I can't hear it," he explained. "Something is not right about this." He looked out at the night-darkened ground. His stomach grumbled. "Hey Norah, how long was I unconscious?"

"Well, time doesn't really mean much to me, but I would say a couple of hours."

"Long enough for it to be night?"

She studied his face, then looked out of the door. "No," she murmured. Alex searched the floor. Finding an old empty bottle, he looked at Norah. She nodded at him. Taking a deep breath, Alex tossed the bottle through the door. For a moment it hovered just across the threshold. Alex quickly threw himself over Norah to protect her from the splintering glass. Then he looked down, to see her feet and torso disappearing through his chest.

"Nice attempt; stupid and useless but it was a very chivalrous thing to do."

"I'll remember that next time," he grumbled. "So any other ideas, smartass?"

"Nope," She was inspecting the barrier, "I think you are trapped here with the rest of us." She looked down at her transparent hand. "Forever trapped," she mumbled.

1953

Norah was awakened by a hard slap to the face. "I did warn you about passing out," Dr. Pryor stated calmly as he glared down at her. The pain had been so intense from the procedure he had been doing on her that the slap's sting seemed almost lost to the rest of her body's screaming pain—almost. Not daring to look down at herself, she searched the area past the doctor. Billy was still there. This eased her heart and broke it at the same time.

He was a mess, with blood and sweat covering his face, but he still tried to smile bravely for her. She wanted to rush to him, comfort him, scream at him, beg him for forgiveness. As if he could hear her thoughts, he mouthed, *not your fault.*

"Oh, my my my, it is not good to lie to the creature," Dr. Pryor chastised calmly. It was then that Norah noticed he had been watching. Pryor twirled a scalpel between his fingers for a moment, then plunged it into Norah's thigh. Through her scream and streaming eyes, she watched the doctor advance on Billy.

"Leave him alone!" she shouted. "There is nothing left of him to torture." Both of Billy's legs now ended at the knee. The flesh at his waist was stripped away to the point that his hip bones showed, glinting white in the surgical lighting. His exposed heart began to beat rapidly inside his ribcage. "Please, let him heal." She screamed, "You have enough of my blood. Let him heal, please."

"I have your blood, yes," Pryor remarked in his even tone. Without looking back at her he continued, "But it is proving increasingly less potent."

"Maybe because you have almost bled her dry," Billy croaked. "Just let her rest for a while and I am sure her blood will regain its potency." Dr. Pryor looked from the syringe to Billy. "Maybe give her something to eat as well. She looks a bit anemic," Billy continued.

"You make several valid points." Pryor scratched at his chin, "You realize, at this point, if I stop administering the blood you will not be able to continue to live?" He spoke as if he were talking over what to prepare for dinner.

"That is okay," Billy gasped, "I mean, I can't say this hasn't been a little slice of heaven—but it hasn't."

Pryor smiled indulgently at Billy's joke. He then turned to Norah. "Should we let you rest?" He asked pleasantly, and his eyebrows rose expectantly. Norah wanted to protest, and her anger flared in her eyes. Pryor smiled slightly.

Looking past the hated physician, she could see Billy pleading silently. Her defiant glare crumbled in defeat. "I think a rest would be good." She couldn't look at either of them now, only at her restrained hands. Her fingertips were blue and red. They were blue from lack of blood and red from clawing at the chair and her restraints. Tears slipped off the end of her nose, falling freely into her lap.

"Very well," Dr. Pryor sighed, walking over to a small grill with a button under it on the wall. "Bring in some meat for the girl," he called through the speaker. Releasing the button, he turned back to Billy. "I think we will be judicious with this batch." His friendly smile was painted on his face. "We should keep you alive long enough to test your theory." He advanced on Billy, kicking one of his leg bones out of the way. Behind him, the door opened. A person slumped into the room carrying a tray. Billy could not see what was happening. He fought back the scream as the burning started in his chest. Red, raw muscle and skin began to form over his exposed heart and lungs. Through streaming eyes, Billy saw the hulking thing that brought in the tray slinking from the room. It stopped. Its eyes met Billy's, and a small sad smile crossed the chapped broken lips. Before Billy could comprehend what had happened, the thing left the room.

A clatter of metal on tile grabbed the Doctor's attention. For the first time, Billy saw anger in Dr. Pryor's eyes. "That fool!" Norah lay on the floor. One foot was still restrained. Billy strained against his leather bindings. Pryor was at the button again. "Who told you to remove her restraints? Get in here this instant." As soon as the button was released, he flew to Norah.

When the doctor's hands were inches away from turning her over, the door opened. So many things happened at once Billy only barely registered it all. Dr. Pryor cried out as a flash of silver reflected the light. Both doctor and syringe fell to the floor, both sending blood across it. The lumbering man lifted Norah off the floor. They both looked at Billy before Norah whispered, "I'm so sorry." Billy screamed as her neck was snapped with such force that her head was nearly ripped off. Now doctor Pryor was screaming, as the beast advanced. Billy screamed Norah's name, knowing she would not answer. The rough hands on either side of his face barely registered. Hot smelly breath stung his ear.

"Better this way," was the last thing Billy heard, other than the creature's cry of pain. Then the world ended.

Dr. Pryor stomped his foot, howling in rage. The steak knife Norah had been given, the one she slashed him with, dripped blood. The spinal cord of the beast-man was severed, but the doctor had been too late to keep him from smashing Billy's skull in. The foot of the beast-man twitched, causing Pryor to kick it as hard as he could. Norah's broken body lay on one side of the room, the two men on the other.

Grabbing whatever he could, he knelt by Norah's corpse. He called through the speaker and two other aberrations entered the room. Norah's body was strung up by the ankles and her throat slit, which caused a moment of panic, as her head separated the rest of the way. It rolled over to rest against Billy's shattered feet. Her sightless eyes stared at the creatures who helped to collect her blood.

Unseen by any of the living, a small girl appeared, white and transparent, next to the mutilated body of Billy. Pearl white tears fell from her eyes as she ran from the room, as far and as fast as she could.

Visitor

"I met him once before, years ago." Chloe stared at the place where Mike's van lights had been. "He came to the Sterben House with a lady." Her eyes were looking into the past. "If I remember correctly, they were quite insulting." Chloe's memories took her back to the first encounter with Mike and Linda. She frowned down at the disc in her hand. "Why would he come to find me now?"

"More importantly," Aaron interrupted, "Who sent him?" Liza looked at him, perplexed. "He said he was sent, and he had done what he was told to do." Aaron's face darkened. "I think I know who sent him."

Chloe's eyes lit up in surprise. "Wait, if Alistair sent him, then—" the realization crashed around her as she ran through the door to the street. "He knows where Alex is." Her tone was defeated; the van was nowhere to be seen. Aaron and Liza hurried to catch up. Liza threw out a hand to stop Aaron. The air around Chloe shimmered like the heat of the desert. Slowly stepping backward, Liza continued to push Aaron behind her.

"Damn it!" Chloe shrieked, stomping the street. The air rippled out from her and the ground broke under her foot. Aaron and Liza were thrown into the air to fall in a tangle several feet away. Liza sat up, pushing Aaron's legs off her. Leaves and twigs continued to tear and fall from swaying trees. Chloe stood in the middle of the road, her head hung in anger.

"What the hell was that?" Aaron whispered.

"She may be corporeal," Liza replied, "But do not underestimate the power of a vengeful spirit." Liza got to her feet. Holding a hand out to Aaron, she gave him a crooked smile, "Or a woman spurned." She pulled him to his feet. "Something to keep in mind." Aaron nodded, wide-eyed and serious.

"I guess we have only one option at the moment." Chloe grumbled as she passed her friends, "Let's find out what is on this disc."

Aaron was surprised that the disc did not spontaneously combust in her hand as she glared at it. A look of fear and concern passed from Aaron to Liza and back. "What would happen if she went full-on vengeful?" Aaron hissed.

"With what we just witnessed," Liza's serious gaze cause Aaron's stomach to tighten, "We don't want to be anywhere near her if that happened."

Aaron stayed a step or two behind Liza as they followed Chloe back to the house. Chloe's agitation at the slow power-up of the TV and disc player made Aaron nervous. Finally, the disc was in and playing. Alistair glared at them from the screen. Aaron was surprised the TV did not melt from the hate radiating from Chloe.

"Chloe Miller," Alistair spat the name, "I would like to extend an invitation to you." He sneered. "I have taken over a certain abandoned hospital." Alistair paused, glaring menacingly at the camera. His expression changed to expectant. His eyes wide, he moved his head in a circular motion.

"What the hell is he doing?" Aaron asked.

"Show the rest of the room, you fool!" Alistair shouted, causing everyone, including the camera user, to jump. Then the view panned across the broken furniture, graffiti-covered walls, and long-neglected floors. Slowly, the shaking picture returned to Alistair's smug face. "In this place, we have dozens of souls." He gestured to the floor, and the camera followed. The shaking intensified. "Some are very recent additions." Linda's motionless body lay on the floor, framed in the middle of the screen. "As you can see, and should already know, I am no stranger to death."

Something moved behind the maniacal wizard. Chloe's attention became laser-focused on the spot. Dropping from the couch, she crawled closer to the TV. She reached behind her, searching for something. "The remote, give me the damned remote!" she shouted. Aaron went to grab it. Before his fingers touched the plastic, it flew into Chloe's hand. Aaron turned. The question on his face was answered by Liz with a frightened shake of her head.

The screen froze and then began to speed backward. The video began to play again. "As you know I am no stranger to death," Alistair repeated, "In fact, we are old friends. So much so that I will assist in helping him claim the souls who stayed behind." Something transparent and panicked appeared in Alistair's grip. Aaron gasped. Liza covered her mouth, her eyes huge with dread. "I will burn—"

The video froze again. Immediately Liza and Aaron began to protest. "Everyone, just calm the hell down!" Chloe shouted. Her voice filled the room resonating in the chests of everyone. Instant silence followed.

Finally, Liza broke the silence. "My god, Chloe, don't you see what is happening?" She pointed at the petrified soul held by Alistair.

"Look!" Chloe shouted, inches away from the screen. She was pointing past Alistair to a doorway.

Aaron looked from the screen to Liza, then back as he shrugged. "What am I supposed to be seeing?" he hissed to Liza.

Returning his shrug, she took a step forward. Squinting, she gasped, "Is it him?".

 Chloe stood up slowly. Turning to face her friend, she smiled as tears ran down her face. Speechless, she could only nod her affirmation. The two women hugged.

Aaron walked past them to get a better look. A smile slowly broke out over his face as he turned to Chloe, "So glad Alex convinced you to get the Super HD TV!" He laughed and pointed to the faces of Alex and Norah watching Alistair from the partially open door behind him.

Experiments

The withered grey creature that was Dr. Pryor happily led Alistair through the halls. "You should have seen this place in its prime. Such a wonder of modern medicine!" He turned to smile at Alistair. The smile left an unsettled feeling in Alistair's stomach as the doctor continued, "Mixed with a fair amount of alchemy." He laughed, "I know what you are thinking, but it is not all about turning base metals into gold." Alistair began to protest. "Of course, you would know that." Pryor looked back apologetically, "Many people, and even the majority of other beings, don't understand its workings."

Alistair began to notice a distinct smell as they reached a shelf in the back of what appeared to have been a staff room. Dr. Pryor hummed as he kept his back to Alistair, who could not see what he was doing. Pryor was humming an old tune from the forties as his arms moved oddly. Metal clanked and clunked into place. Surfaces scraped and scratched until a loud bam shuddered through the floor.

"I must apologize." Pryor smiled sheepishly as he handed Alistair a flashlight. "It seems the power company wants to be paid." A pale beam of light barely illuminated the step in front of Dr. Pryor as he descended into the darkness. Alistair was about to cast a lighting spell, but tears welled up in his eyes from the stench of death wafting from the blackness. Gagging, he invoked a protection spell to cut out the smell, then he cast the light. As the stairway and hall below instantly illuminated, Dr. Pryor stepped up to Alistair. He was clapping his hands lightly and smiled, the dry skin of his face drawing tightly across his sharp cheekbones.

It's like four inches of skin stretched over twelve inches of the skull! Alistair thought. Dr. Pryor turned cheerily, marveling at the light. Alistair watched the bare patch on the back of Pryor's head descend further. As he followed, he realized the bald patch wasn't merely a bald area, but that he was looking at a bare skull. The skin of his head seemed to have just been worn away. I'm following a living corpse, Alistair mused. Then, at the bottom of the stairs, Alistair's eyes widened in shock.

Dr. Pryor's calm demeanor suddenly changed, like ice cream melting in a hot pan. In a flash, he pulled a long metal pole from a stand near the wall and swung it above his head. Bringing it down with surprising strength, Pryor shouted. Metal clanged and sparks flew where the pole hit the cement floor. Along the walls, chained and huddled, were more than twenty beasts. They looked like crosses between humans and… wolves or panthers. Some had horns like bulls, while others represented sheep. Blood began to seep toward Alistair's shoe. It spread, encountered his shield, and flowed past. Following the small stream to its source, even Alistair's shriveled heart stirred.

A gaping wound bleed freely from the head of a giant creature that was part man and part alligator. It whimpered and cowered before the evil physician. "So that you always remember your failure," Pryor spat as he hefted the pole up to clear the blood from the end. "So sorry you had to witness that," Pryor's pleasant tone returned. "At one time he was my most trusted creation." A sigh escaped, "That is, until he nearly allowed an escape." He took a sharp step toward the cringing creature. Flinching, it pulled as far from the doctor as its chain would allow.

"So, what happened to the one that tried to escape?"

"Oh, it was utterly destroyed." Pryor smiled happily, leading the way further into the room. "Can't have it encouraging the others, now could we?"

"Defiantly not."

Nodding his approval at Alistair's words, Dr. Pryor held open a door. "Let's discuss how we can help each other." Alistair walked into a richly appointed office. Dark wooden paneling and furniture sat below a gorgeous exposed beam ceiling. Between the beams were ornate metal panels. "Pool?" Dr. Pryor waved his hand over a beautiful table covered in rich red felt.

Waiting

Alex had never been a fan of waiting for others. Waiting, trapped, and hungry were not what he considered a good time. A sound like angry dogs wrestling a bear escaped his stomach. "What the hell was that?" Norah asked, stepping away from Alex as if he would implode, or try to eat her.

"Sorry," he grumbled, "but unlike you, I still need to eat." Hunger was making him grumpy, but he immediately knew he was being extremely rude. "Sorry, that was uncalled for."

She was staring at him, her face unreadable. "Yeah, it's been a long time." Her head tilted toward a shoulder. "I think… well, I don't want to get your hopes up." She glanced at him quickly. "Probably better to not have mentioned it. Sorry."

"Um, sorry what?"

"Well, at some point they put in a fallout shelter." She was looking at him, but past him. "It was all stocked up in case something happened." She seemed to be trying to make up her mind.

"Sounds like something we should investigate. Have you been there before?"

Again, she was not looking at him as she chewed on her bottom lip. "It's been a long time," she whispered.

"There might be something," Alex's stomach protested again. "Water would be amazing, even."

"I don't know if it is a good idea to wander around, with your wizard friend and Doctor Evil here." Alex snickered, and she raised an eyebrow.

He waved her off as he composed himself. "Sorry, it was a character in a movie." Alex smiled. Frowning at him, she began to return the way they had come. "No wait, please. I am sorry."

She paused as he reached out to her. "I guarantee nothing." Norah's eyes flashed dangerously. "We have to go past the morgue, and that is not a pleasant place at the best of time." She steeled her nerves. "Remember I told you about the ones in the basement?"

"You mentioned them, but honestly you never told me anything about them," Alex hissed as he followed Norah. She was moving quickly. Suddenly she turned, disappearing through a wall. Alex stopped short, frowning. Norah popped back out, sending Alex stumbling back.

"Don't do that!"

"Sorry, forgot you had a body."

"Nice," he grumbled as Norah passed completely through the wall. Motioning him to follow, she glided further away. "Chloe was never this annoying."

"I can hear you," she sang as she turned a corner. At least he hoped she turned a corner, and hadn't just got annoyed and slipped through the wall again. Hurrying to catch up, he nearly collided with her at the top of more stairs.

"How many staircases are in this place?" Alex huffed.

"You know, I've never counted, but now that you mention it, there does seem to be a lot." She frowned. "Some of them go to all the floors, some only to certain ones, still others only go from the top floor to the courtyard."

"That is kinda weird, don't you think?" He frowned.

"Up until now, I never thought of it. But you are correct. That is odd." Norah stood deep in thought until Alex's stomach growled again. "Right, some sort of food for the living." Without a look back at Alex, she began to glide down the stairs.

"I'm standing right here," he mumbled, "and I have a name!" he called to her retreating back.

"That's nice," floated up to his ears. After the first landing, she was hovering in the space between the stairways as they turned. "We are heading down to the basement," she informed him, sinking through the empty air as he descended. He lost sight of her as he turned on the landings, his feet thudding and crunching on the concrete, trash, and fallen plaster as he followed. He hurried down the flights, jumping the last two.

"Once we get there, you need to be very quiet. I think you'll be safe." She paused. Alex flew past her as his momentum carried him. He had to grab the handrail to stop. As soon as he did, she began to descend again. "I know *I'm* safe." She glanced at him, "I mean, you can't eat a ghost, so I'll be fine."

"Wait, what?" Alex demanded.

"I think you'll be okay. He generally only eats the dead." She glanced back at him before disappearing down another level. "It has been a while since we have had anyone die here." Her voice echoed. Alex ran to keep up, jumping the rail and landing next to her on the ground floor. Alex bent over, hand on knees, trying to catch his breath.

"Oh," she exclaimed causing him to look up, "that lady, the one the wizard killed?" Wide-eyed he stared at her. "Maybe he ate her. Yeah, that is what probably happened." She smiled, clapping her hands once. "You'll be fine." With a happy bounce, she turned and disappeared through a door.

"Who just ate!?" Alex called slamming through the doors to follow. "You said it was safe earlier! Wait!"

The Message

"Yes!" Chloe pumped up a fist in the air. "Now let's find out where he is!" Her face darkened, "And let's finish this crap with Alistair." Glasses rattled in the kitchen. Aaron looked back, worried. Liza noted his tension. Touching his arm reassuringly, she tried to smile. It came out looking pained. Aaron was not comforted.

They started the video over. Chloe's face contorted in a frown as she watched Alistair's spectacle. "Chloe Miller," a sharp intake of collective breath like a hiss filled the room, "You may think you have defeated me, but as you can see, I escaped your feeble trap." Chloe's fists clenched. "My plans have changed. I no longer need Constance to—"Chloe's attention darted to the movement behind Alistair Fox. She smiled at Alex as he and the young woman disappeared behind a door. "So as you can see, I have taken over this place and the souls within are mine to destroy." Chloe returned her attention to Alistair's eyes.

"I wonder, who's the girl?" Aaron asked. Liza glared at him. Aaron immediately closed his mouth. Chloe's head tilted slightly. Liza's displeasure was not lost on Aaron.

"Ya daft fool! As if she doesn't have enough to worry about." She admonished in a hiss.

"I'm not worried about Alex being unfaithful." Chloe exhaled as if exhausted.

"Idiot!" Liza slapped Aaron on the back of the head. Before he could say a word, Chloe hushed them.

"So, if you don't come to face me, I will burn out every soul in this place." Alistair finished smugly, his face full of malice.

"How in the hell did he escape?" Liza demanded.

"That is a very fine question," a gravely, familiar voice answered. Aaron shouted in fright and Liza growled, while Chloe groaned. "Is that any way to treat an old friend?" Kerlvin asked through a wicked smile.

"Old friend?" Aaron stammered. "There is no way I would consider a demon a friend."

"There is no reason to be insulting," Kerlvin sighed in exasperation. "I happen to be an arch-demon."

"Well, congratu-fu—" Aaron began, but Chloe's shush broke in, "—lations," he finished lamely.

"Thank you." Kerlvin bowed.

"Why are you here?" Chloe asked, rolling the annoyance out of her shoulders, "Again?"

"Careful, dear Chloe, I might misunderstand," his face split in an evil grin, "and think you are not happy to see me."

"There is no misunderstanding," Liza interrupted, "we are less than happy to see you." Her hand waved toward the screen that still held a frozen picture of Alistair. "How did you let this bastard escape?"

"I don't believe I like your accusing tone," Kerlvin frowned.

"How do you explain Alistair out and about on earth?" Aaron joined in. "Oh don't tell me," his hand slapped his forehead, "twin evil brother? No wait, eviler twin?" Liza's hand softly pushed Aaron away from the clearly annoyed demon.

Kerlvin's eyes narrowed dangerously. "There may have been extenuating circumstances," He explained through a growl. Through gritted teeth, he continued, "We have a bigger problem." He paused dramatically. He waited expectantly. Chloe's attention was fixed to the image of Alistair, while Liza and Aaron muttered quietly between them. "I said—"

"We heard what you said," Chloe interrupted, "I just don't see how your problems are our problems." The fierceness of her glare matched the demon's. "Extenuating circumstances? He had help, didn't he?"

Kerlvin held her gaze for a moment. The fire behind his eyes died as his wings drooped. "Yes, it was Simon."

"That little basketball-shaped bastard!" Aaron shouted.

"It is worse than you think." Kerlvin's shoulders sagged. "Alistair is at Saint Mary's Hospital outside of Coudersport."

"It doesn't matter where it is," Chloe turned to face the others, "we are going, we're getting Alex back, and we're putting Alistair in the ground or in hell."

"And you are not going to fail this time! The place doesn't matter." Liza seethed, and energy crackled in her hands. Kerlvin met her posturing with fire erupting in the palm of his left hand while his right gripped the hilt of a jewel-encrusted sword.

"Um, no, actually it kinda does matter," Aaron interrupted, moving between Kerlvin and Liza, earning him Liza's ire. Holding up his hands, Aaron gave her an apologetic look. Liza growled but let the energy evaporate. Blowing out the tension, he continued, "Saint Mary's was closed after it was discovered they were hiding the bodies of patients who died." He ignored Liza's flared nostrils, which seemed to be emitting smoke. Aaron imagined Liza as part dragon. His smirk was wiped from his face by the look he received from Chloe. A little shake got his mind back on track.

"They had a contract with the state and the VA." He glanced at Kerlvin, who was looking past him to Liza. "They got paid as long as they continued to care for patients who had no one to pay for them." Chloe's expression said *so?* "Well, the problem was, they kept people on the rolls when they died and simply disposed of the bodies. They burned them or buried them in a meadow behind the hospital." Aaron was trying to remember the details. "I guess they developed the area at some point and that is when the bones started showing up." He looked around at the unimpressed faces. "Hey, it was a big deal several years ago. I think they were still finding bodies until like two years ago."

"That is sad and all, but what relevance does it have to beating the tar out of Alistair?" Chloe demanded.

"Well, um, I'm getting there." Aaron faltered, "They are pretty sure they have not found all of the bodies. Many of the ones that had died had families that were looking for them, people who thought they were still alive." Sadness crept over his features.

"Not to be insensitive, but how does that relate to anything?" Chloe demanded. The air around her began to shimmer. Aaron looked to Liza for guidance. A smile began to creep over Kerlvin's face.

Liza approached Chloe. Speaking carefully and calmly, she explained, "Sometimes spirits who are left behind who are lost, or forgotten, tend to get angry." Chloe turned to glare at her. Aaron and Kerlvin took a step back. Aaron's face held fear, while Kerlvin held a hopeful fascination. "I know you were upset when *you* were dead," Liza spoke softly. Aaron wasn't sure this was the best way to handle Chloe. Her annoyance seemed to grow. Kerlvin licked his lips hungrily. "But you see—"

Aaron cringed and panic overtook him. "Chloe, calm down before you become a vengeful spirit and kill us all," he pleaded.

"Oh sure, take all the fun out of the moment," Kerlvin pouted. Liza jumped back, throwing her hands over her head.

Chloe looked at each face. She saw fear, and Kerlvin's black glassy eyes, which held disappointment. "But I'm alive again," she whispered.

"Yes, yes, you are alive, but you were dead longer than you were alive. When you came back you retained many of your spectral powers," Kerlvin explained as he paced grumpily, "including the nuclear option."

"Nuclear option?" Chloe's confusion was evident as she repeated the unfamiliar words.

"He just means you could explode in anger like a huge bomb," Liza explained.

"So, you think the ghosts there might go…nuclear? Good, they can take out Alistair while we save Alex."

"Oh my God," Kerlvin buried his face in his hands, "No! The ghosts have no power against Alistair. There was something else going on in the hospital that no one knew about." Kerlvin glared at Aaron's raised eyebrows, "What? I said God? Remind me to explain the relationship between God and the demons to you one day."

His face soured. "The guy running the place became known to us," Kerlvin explained, flapping his black leathery wings and coming to rest on the couch. Chloe sat at the far end, listening. "He came into possession of a certain item and he began to experiment on…" he scratched at the small black beard as he chose his words, "non-humans, and oh dear God, Aaron, if you ask if that means animals, I will destroy you for the sake of your friends."

"What do you mean?" Aaron demanded, "I know what non-humans are. It is not like you and the basketball are the only things we've ever come across."

"Enough," Chloe yelled, "Kerlvin, no smiting. Aaron, don't antagonize the demon. Liza, stop laughing!" Everyone turned to see Liza failing to hide her mirth. "What kind of experiments, and how did you find out about them?"

"Ah, well, this might cause a little bit of a stir." Kerlvin explained uncomfortably, "There is a ghoul in the hospital. He has been giving us information for years." The statement was met with silence. Looks of disgust covered Liza and Aaron's faces, matching the confusion on Chloe's.

Seeing her expression, Liza explained, "Ghouls are disgusting creatures. They are eaters of the dead." Now all of the living wore the same disgust. Her attention turned to Kerlvin, her tone accusing, "Just what did you promise this ghoul so it would help you?" Kerlvin looked at her with the least convincing shocked face he could. Before he could answer, she demanded, "What did you offer the beast?'

Her shout turned Kerlvin's acting into frustrated anger. "Your prejudice is only outstripped by your ignorance," he spat. Lightning crackled in Liza's hand, yet Kerlvin looked at her with disappointment.

"Clearly there is more to this story," Chloe stepped between the two, "but I think you have forgotten that we need to get Alex back and destroy Alistair. You need to tell us what we are up against."

"And what kind of experiments the ghoul was doing," Aaron added.

"It wasn't the ghoul, it was the doctor—" Kerlvin shook his head, eyeing Aaron. "Just one blast, or maybe send him into another dimension?" he asked.

"As tempting as that sometimes is," Liza grudgingly admitted, "no, just tell us about the experiments." She sighed. Aaron was annoyed at the agreement of the witch and demon, and especially the small entertained smile from Chloe. It disappeared in a blink.

"You appear to have left out some pretty important information," Chloe suggested. "When do you plan on telling us what has been going on?"

"It is not something we are proud of." Kerlvin shrugged.

"And you are still withholding!" Chloe's hand flew into the air. "There is something worse than Alistair here and Simon seems to have teamed up with it!" She turned back to the demon, daring him to deny it.

"First of all," Kerlvin started maneuvering away from all of the accusing glares. "Yes, I knew what had gone on there." He held up a hand to quell the protests, "But the good doctor had not been active for years. Not since the place closed." Kerlvin seemed to be trying to tiptoe around the subject.

"What exactly *was* going on?" Their stares of revulsion did not seem to bother Kerlvin, but he ardently avoided Chloe's gaze."

"You think the reason this hospital took in so many charity cases was because they wanted the money from the care?" Kerlvin laughed humorlessly. "Humans always want to think it is about money." He shook his head. "This place was run by someone more evil than anything you have ever come across." He addressed Chloe directly. "I think you may have been the inspiration for all of this."

"Don't you dare blame anything on me." Chloe growled, "Stop beating around the bush and tell us what was going on!"

"Fine, since you seem to want the whole story." Kerlvin made himself comfortable. Liza sat on a stool by the kitchen counter while Aaron dragged a chair loudly across the tile floor. Kerlvin spared him a look of disgust before starting his story.

Dr. Pryor's Path

1944, Hurtgen Forest

Medic Sargent Pryor shook from the cold and fear. He could hear the cries of the wounded calling out for him. Swallowing his fear, he grabbed his bag and ran from the foxhole. He found two soldiers who had already succumbed to their wounds and the cold. He was able to patch up one young man, his buddies helping him to safety. Pryor next came upon one of those scenes that would be forever burned into his memory. There had been so many of these that this one barely registered at first. This time he found a soldier blown apart. Missing limbs, grievous wounds, blood staining the snow. Pryor was about to move on when he heard labored breathing. He was shocked to see the soldier's wounds begin to heal. Before he could get an explanation, the solider looked at Pryor, who stared back. In an instant, the soldier began to change into a wolf. Fully healed, the beast ran off, disappearing into the woods.

1945, Outside Bergen-Belsen

The elite SS unit had decimated Sergeant Pryor's unit. In the end, Pryor and three other men were still alive. Having defeated the enemy, he sat against a bombed-out house, watching the others. Pryor looked at his companions in disgust as they looted the corpses. That is, until they found the box. Thinking it might have military value, he checked the contents. Ancient books mixed with files and journals. He recognized many as medical documents. Having learned a little German growing up, he could read some of the documents. What they contained entranced him. His thoughts took him back several months, to the badly injured soldier who had lived despite the loss of so much of his body.

Pryor heard the damaged staff car roar to life. He watched as his companions began to loot a house. There was no way they were going to let him take up space with the large box. A dead SS Lieutenant Coronel stared up at him. The man's hat lay nearby. Pryor stared at the skull on the cap, and it stared back. Pryor undid the soldier's gun belt, took out the Luger, and placed the belt with its long dagger into the box, next to the officer's cap. He loaded a round into the chamber of the weapon and calmly walked up to the staff car. The other two men's faces held happy, greedy grins, even as the bullets passed through their brains. Pryor stood over one of the men, a private whose name he had never learned. The man's eyes were open and moving. Pryor studied the face. Blood and brain were splayed out behind the man, but he was not dead yet. Intrigued, Pryor returned to the box, placing the gun inside. He withdrew the dagger. The fear in those eyes was most exhilarating as he plunged the dagger deep into the man's heart. Even then, the man fought to survive. Pryor knew then that this was his reason for being. He had to learn how to live forever.

1953, Saint Mary's Hospital

Former Combat Medic Pryor was the newest doctor at the well-known hospital. Few knew of his combat experience, only that he had been to war. It must have been for that reason he'd had so many of the unnamed, horribly wounded soldiers transferred there. The rumor was that he was trying to heal these unfortunate souls. They had the most horrifying wounds—head wounds, arms, legs and faces missing—all should have been killed by their injuries, yet they were here, and alive. He spent many of his free hours alone with the men. He studied the old books and tried different treatments, attempting to understand the will to survive. He translated the German files. They told about experiments run at the camps. Frustrated, he needed more test subjects.

1968, Saint Mary's Hospital

As the Head Surgeon, Pryor rarely stepped foot into the hospital. He had been instrumental in securing the state contract that allowed for the free treatment of the homeless and orphaned, all subsidized by the government. Looking around the stark white tile walls under the hum of fluorescent lights, Dr. Pryor smiled. Walking the hall, he noted that the screams and cries of his patients were barely audible. He stopped to look through the thick glass of a heavy steel door. His reflection looked younger every time he saw it. The creature in the room twisted and contorted in agony. Dr. Pryor frowned, making a note on his clipboard. Taking a deep breath, he continued on to the rooms of his sanctuary hidden below the hospital.

1996, Saint Mary's Hospital

He was still amused that no one questioned him. They just accepted, or assumed, he was his own son. He followed in his father's footsteps, they would say. The only thing that troubled him was his uneasy partnership with the coroner. There was something about Winston that bothered Dr. Pryor, but as long as he did not question where half of the bodies went, their arrangement would stay acceptable.

2002, Saint Mary's Hospital

Dr. Pryor sat in his beautifully appointed office under the hospital, watching the news. Police were raiding the hospital offices. Several doctors and nurses were led out in handcuffs, as digging continued behind the building. Dr. Pryor was sure Winston would be the next one led away. "How interesting that would be," Dr. Pryor mused. He had discovered what Winston was not too long before all the trouble began coming to light. A ghoul as a coroner; really, quite brilliant. He laughed. No one wanted to be down there in the morgue, so Winston could spend as much time as he wanted to have a meal.

Since the closure of the hospital, Dr. Pryor had to deal with less than ideal subjects for his work. The only ones who wandered in were wayward teens and the homeless. Now drug users were his new crop, and they were mostly disappointing. So few of the "others" would show up. Oh well, these were just different hurdles to overcome. "A corrupted soul is still useful, is it not?" he questioned the terrified young man strapped to the table. "We'll find out just how much it takes to remove it completely." Screams filled the operating theater.

"So, he finds some Nazi spell books and that turns him into a messed up Dr. Moreau?" Aaron asked disgustedly.

"Nice reference!" Chloe commended.

Kerlvin rolled his eyes. "No," Kerlvin blew out a frustrated breath, "I am saying his discovery of non-humans and their ability to survive, together with the books and files he found, led him to what is happening now." Kerlvin 's attention was on Liza, who returned the gaze with disgust.

"Don't blame me for this!" Liza shouted. "Our magic is not evil! In fact, most non-humans are your kind."

"My kind?" Kerlvin demanded, offended.

"You spiteful, evil creature," Liza shouted. "Your kind introduced evil into the world!"

"Oh, really!" Kerlvin shouted, his black wings flapping, raising him into the air. The blast stung their eyes and skin. "I'm the bad guy in all of this?": His anger boomed through the room, "*My* kind did not write the books, we did not create the science. We did not condone the experiments. That was all on you *humans*." His black claw pointed at Liza, then swung to include them all. "Witches and wizards translated the magic, learned to call us, grasped at power—"

"Yes, and you were more than happy to oblige!" Liza shouted. "More than happy to make a deal for their souls."

"Their souls were already ours!" Kerlvin shouted. Fire flew from his fingers and off his wings and horns. "They gave them freely through their own desires and corruption, long before they discovered us. Without us to temper their learning, to temper their gaining of power, this world would be a smoking cinder." The heat radiating off the demon began to blister the paint. "We stood back once, to see how far you humans would go." The walls and ceiling around Kerlvin began to blacken. "We thought the first time the world fought that would be enough." Smoke turned to flame, then back to smoke, ready to ignite. "You fools didn't learn, so we stepped back again." His voice held loathing, "You nearly destroyed everything—millions dead, and the advent of nuclear proliferation. We barely were able to stop it! The combined power of the two kingdoms nearly failed!" Suddenly the fire was out. Kerlvin's feet slapped onto the floor. His face contorted into an embarrassed yet malicious glare. "Never mind that now. We," he shook his head angrily, "*you* have a maniac to stop." In a blast of sulfur and heat, Kerlvin was gone.

"What the hell was that all about?" Aaron demanded.

"I don't really know," Liza muttered quietly. She cast a spell to repair the damage caused by the demon's outburst.

"I think we are on our own for the moment," Chloe sighed. She was on her feet with her jacket in hand before the other two knew what had happened. "Come on, it is a long drive to Saint Mary's."

Visit to the Black

"That's not a good sign," Norah muttered as they spied the bloody remains of Linda still lying face down in the lobby. Closing the door silently on the scene, Norah paused, uncertainty evident as she chewed her lower lip. "Still," she looked Alex up and down, sizing him up, "I don't think he'd be interested—but then again, what do I know?" She shrugged. "Come on."

"Whoa, hold on one damn minute!" Alex hissed, grabbing Norah's upper arm. "You need to start explaining where we are going and what you mean about something not eating me!" Huffing through his frustration, he continued, "I appreciate you know more about this place than I ever will, but you need to start telling me what the hell is going on." Alex got the impression of the spoiled girls from back in high school as Norah rolled her eyes and huffed.

"Fine," and the look on her face entertained and annoyed Alex all at once. "This place has a past." She glared at him for a moment. He looked back with a calm expression that said *continue.* "You really want to get into this now?" She frowned and waited. Alex did not say anything, just crossed his arms and held the polite inquisitive look. "Wow, this Chloe must have the patience of a saint," she grumbled. "All right then, fine." Throwing her hands up in resignation, she began to descend the stairs. "Back when this place was an actual hospital, they took in all kinds of hard-luck cases." She hesitated on the third step down. Alex noticed it too. The darkness felt blacker here. In other places in the hospital, the shadows would slowly engulf an area, but here, at the bottom of the stairs, there was a razor's edge separating gloom from pitch black. He knew it was unnatural. This was something he and Chloe had seen before. It was the work of spirits who couldn't or wouldn't leave the shadows. This knowledge did not make it any less terrifying.

"I've only been down here a couple of times," Norah whispered. "The first time was shortly after I was first admitted." A smirk crossed her face. "I was messing around with Billy." She frowned at the snicker from Alex. "It was nothing like that! Although…" Several thoughts ran through her mind. Shaking the thoughts away, she said, "He was supposed to keep watch on me. Well, I couldn't stand being bored, so I used to sneak out of the ward and hide." The smile she wore became strained. "I wish I had never done that. Maybe it wouldn't have…" Her thoughts clouded her eyes. "Anyway," she stood straight and wiped all emotion away, "I had exhausted everywhere to hide in the ward, so I had started venturing further and further out." Alex noticed they had only descended one more step. He couldn't tell if she was stalling on purpose, or just didn't realize as she spoke. "So, one night I ended up down here. I heard a couple of other girls in the ward talking about the fallout shelter and, well, some of their ideas for its use." The smirk had returned. "So I thought maybe when Billy found me, we might…" her blush was obvious even with her transparent skin, "explore the shelter." She immediately sped on. "I was down here, and even then, it was darker than the rest of the hospital. I know it was night, but there was less light and far more shadow than there should have been." Taking a step backward, Norah advanced one more stair. "I guess I knew something was wrong, I mean, I felt it right away. You know, my kind can sense each other."

Alex was intrigued, but seriously wanted to find some water. His throat felt like sandpaper as he breathed. "Wait, you were already dead by this point?" Alex scratched his head.

"No," she laughed. "I did meet my first ghost that night, though—but I mean others like *me*."

Alex still wore a perplexed expression. "Are you a witch?" he perked up as he asked, but he immediately regretted his question at the look he received. The air seemed colder, but he wasn't sure if it was the area or Norah's glare.

"I am not a witch," she growled. Then her expression changed. Alex was amazed at how fast her emotions switched. "Do you know a witch? Have you met one?"

"Yeah, she is Chloe's maid of honor," Alex replied. His feet were starting to hurt from standing on the stairs for so long. "So yeah, I know a witch." Norah's head cocked to the side as if she was trying to decide if he was lying. "I know a couple of demons too, if you are interested." Alex frowned.

His statement froze Norah faster than the cold that seemed to be seeping from the walls. "You are in league with demons?" Norah asked, her eyes darting behind Alex. He realized she was looking for a way to escape.

"No! No, they are not friends. I mean one helped us, but I think it was more to help himself. Then he brought his buddy along, who had made a deal with Alistair, the wizard, and well, we ended up fighting together to banish Alistair. But obviously, it didn't work, so—" Alex shut his mouth tight. The look he was getting, and the fact that she was slowly edging into the wall, told him he had over-shared. "Damn it." Alex rubbed his hand over his stubble. "Kerlvin is a right pain in the ass. We are not in league with him. We only cooperate because Alistair is worse."

"Lesser of two evils, huh?"

Alex sighed. At least she wasn't trying to disappear anymore. "I was always warned to stay away from demons." She looked a little confused. "They are known to use us." Her confusion shifted into discomfort. "When they are done, they drag us to hell." She hugged herself as she shuddered. Looking directly into Alex's eyes, she begged, "I don't want to go to hell."

"Whoa! I won't let that happen. But," he had to know, "I still don't know what you mean by those like you?"

"Oh well, you know," she shrugged, "I mean a monster. Well, what you would call a monster." The corner of her mouth twitched as Alex took a step backward up a stair. "I'm a lycanthrope, and so were my parents and my sister." Alex's foot paused between steps, then slowly descended. "That is why Dr. Pryor wanted me here. Sometimes it skips a generation, and other times it just manifests late. I was the latter." Her eyes searched the past. "It is bad when it happens late. I would spontaneously transform." A shudder ran through her again. "It hurt so bad, I had no control over my body." She whispered, "My dad had heard that Dr. Pryor knew about our kind and could help. I have no idea who told him that." Hatred darkened her eyes. "Why my sister had to come along that night—" tears welled up and rolled down her cheeks. "It just happened; I must have thrashed out. I killed them all." Her voice was now barely a whisper, "Billy always tried to tell me it wasn't my fault." Norah looked defiantly back at Alex as if he had suggested it was. "I know it wasn't my fault. Dad was tricked to bringing me here. The only one at fault is that bastard Pryor." Spinning on her heel, she descended into the dark.

"Um, I'm really sorry about all of that, but," Alex followed her into the black, "that still doesn't tell me who the hell is going to eat me!"

"Oh, right." She stopped so suddenly that Alex walked through her. "Winston—he's a ghoul."

Are We There Yet?

Aaron glanced sideways at Chloe who was staring out the front window of the car. He checked over his shoulder at Liza, who was engrossed in an ancient-looking book. Returning his attention to the front. his eyes darted to the speedometer. "Um, Chloe," he forced a calm he didn't feel into his voice, "Liza is basically immortal, and you've been dead," he faltered at her frown, "but I have neither of your experiences, so could we slow down a little?" Chloe didn't even look over at him, but her foot did ease up slightly on the accelerator. Blowing out a bit of his stress, Aaron began to chew on his thumb.

"What is the problem?" Liza sighed.

"What? No problems here," Aaron shrugged.

"You always chew on your thumb when you are nervous or anxious." Liza began.

"Or awake," Chloe finished for her. "Alex is not nearly as fidgety."

"Oh, he's rather fidgety, love," Liza commented, "You're just too much in love to notice. Give it a year or two, and those cute little habits will make you want to stab him." Liza chuckled. "Repeatedly."

"Something I should know?" Aaron asked nervously.

"Oh no, dear," Liza smirked.

Chloe could feel the tension in the car. Even though they were doing their best to make it feel normal, she could tell they were worried. "I appreciate the thought," Chloe said as she took a corner and sent Liza and Aaron sliding. "I know you are worried too."

"Yes, but we can't help Alex," Aaron grunted pushing himself off the passenger side door, "if we are dead. Chloe, slow down, or let me drive."

"I thought you wanted to get there alive," Liza asked. Again, Chloe let up on the pedal. A battered sign told them they were about thirty miles from the town. Aaron began looking at his phone, while Liza brought out an old map. "Did you find the hospital?"

"No. Did you say it was on a mountain road?" Aaron's face reflected the phone's screen. Liza conjured up a dim light as she looked at her map.

"I've got it, just not sure where it is with the new roads." Liza frowned. Aaron contorted in his seat to hold his phone next to the map. "Is there a problem?" The car was slowing to a stop.

"Aaron being all pretzeled like that is making me uncomfortable," Chloe said, pulling her hands off the wheel. Her fingers ached from holding on so tight. "Just work together to get us there." Chloe hissed, "This road is—" Aaron opened his door and immediately felt it. Quickly jumping to open the backseat door, he spun to look into the blackness. Something was moving in the trees, and he could hear its heavy breathing. A twig snapped. Aaron clambered into the back seat, slamming and locking the door quickly. All three agreed silently to hurry on their way. Chloe's eyes darted to the rearview mirror. She saw something large for an instant in the red of the taillights, and when she looked again it was gone.

Aaron handed his phone to Liza, as his hands shook too hard to be of use. "What the hell was that?" Aaron shouted. "It was huge and, and, hairy. Holy shit! Did we just see bigfoot?"

"No." Liza closed her eyes and felt the air. "That was something else. Something," her eyes shot open, "something in pain." Carefully rechecking the map, she yelped in victory, "Got it! Take the next turn, and then slow down. It might be hard to see. Yes, here. Okay, this will take us all the way to Saint Mary's." As they drove, the woods felt like they were closing in, forming a tunnel of blackness. The chill of sorrow seeped in through every gap. Chloe turned on the heater to fight the encroaching cold.

Aaron and Liza braced against the seats. Chloe's foot hit the brakes hard. The old forgotten building seemed to explode out of the darkness. Its crumbling weed-strewn circular drive took them straight to the front door. Chloe eased the car closer.

"I can honestly say," Liza whispered, "be it a dungeon, castle, or prison, I've never felt this kind of foreboding."

"I don't know what I expected," Chloe said, edging forward to look up through the windshield, "but it is bigger than I thought."

"Nine floors," Aaron counted, "along with east and west wings. Although I doubt that he is in the west wing, as there is very little left of it." Aaron pointed to the collapsed roof and obvious fire damage.

Chloe rolled slowly up to the front entrance along the curved drive. The three steps up to the doors were crumbling, with small plants growing through the cracks. The front doors were chained shut. Upon closer inspection, however, they could see the glass and boards that had covered it shattered and strewn around.

"Man, this looks daunting." Aaron looked up the building through his window.

Closing her eyes, Chloe inhaled through her nose. "I know, but Alex is in there." She stepped out of the car without hesitation. As everyone exited the car, their doors banged shut, too loudly. Chloe cringed at the sound like it was something rude. "I was told to always be quiet around a hospital," she whispered.

"That would only matter if there was someone here that needed to rest." Aaron frowned. "Only ones here need to be laid to rest." His attempt at a joke earned him a slap to the back of his head from Liza. Chloe looked at the others, shrugged, and ducked through the broken doors. Aaron protested, but was the first to follow.

The look of the lobby sickened Chloe. Between the wanton destruction and the foul graffiti, she could barely imagine what it might have looked like when it was a functioning hospital. Moving past the battered reception station, she stopped in confusion. The lobby couch and the area around it were clean and pristine. "That is weird," she muttered.

"Alistair," Liza frowned, feeling the remnants of magic. "Come on," and they continued to head toward the double doors and the hall Chloe had seen Alex down. Suddenly the ancient intercom system crackled into life, causing them to crouch and look for the source of the sound.

"Welcome, Chloe. So happy you accepted my invitation," Alistair's voice taunted. "I have some friends that are very much looking forward to eating— oh, I meant *meeting* you." His voice echoed through the empty halls for a moment before silence fell.

"If that was supposed to be scary, all I can say is, *lame*." Chloe frowned.

"Good use of the slang," Aaron smiled, giving her two thumbs up.

The Morgue

Norah hesitated as she made the final step down into the basement. This was the only the third time she had been down here. A shudder ran up her spine. She hoped Alex didn't notice. "Are we there? It doesn't look like anything." His voice barely a whisper as he tried to see through the gloom. His only light was the faint glow from Norah.

"This is it; this was the morgue," she replied with a calm she did not feel. The memories came flooding back. This was the place where she had met the screaming man.

She had snuck out of her ward, as she had told Alex, but in truth, she was trying to find somewhere to be alone. Billy had recently given her the battered stuffed wolf her sister had always carried. It was cleaner than she remembered. Trying to block the thought of what Billy must have cleaned off sent her on her quest for solitude. She was sitting in a stairwell, letting her tears fall onto the toy's matted fur, when she heard a door open. Knowing it was more trouble than she wanted to deal with, Norah quietly descended the stairs. She pushed through the first set of doors she came to.

Norah had just ducked under the two oval windows of the door when it happened. The room got deathly cold. Turning slowly at a sound coming from behind her, fear filled Norah. Suddenly a man emerged through the wall of huge metal drawers. She shivered even now as she saw him in her mind's eye.

He was naked and covered in blood. There were holes in his chest that seemed to be ceaselessly flowing crimson. On one side of his head was a small hole, on the other side, half of his scalp was missing. He stood in the dim light, pointing at her, screaming. She could still hear that anguished, terrible scream of pain, confusion, and anger.

Norah remembered running blindly. She made it to the second floor, where she began pulling on locked doors, screaming for help. Billy was the one who found her. He had calmed her down and hidden her in a closet. She told her story into his chest as he awkwardly rubbed her back. When she finished, she had expected the worst. Yet he hadn't laughed or called her crazy, just nodded understandingly.

"There are things in this place that no one should see," Billy told her gruffly. "Never mind that, let's get you back to your ward." Billy shook the gloom from his voice as he held her at arm's length. Norah smiled, relieved, until suddenly the smile slid from her face.

"Horo! Horo! Where is Horo?" Norah cried. In her haste to escape the basement, she had lost her sister's stuffed wolf. The wolf had given her a sense of security since arriving. Norah felt the comfort of a family when she held the toy to her heart. If she closed her eyes, she could see her parents and her sister smiling at her, comforting her.

"Where did you have him last?" Billy asked seriously. He knew the importance of the item even more than she did. He had sewn a small pouch into the toy. It was a medicine bag he placed there in hopes of added protection for her.

Norah let go to search around her feet, panic building by the second. "I left him. I left him with the bloody man," she screeched.

"Then you and I will go to retrieve him." Billy spoke calmly, taking her hand. Her fear fought with her desire to reunite with Horo, and mixed with the electricity of his hand in hers. At the top of the stairs, she pulled back against his grip. Pulling her hand free, all Norah could do was hug herself and shudder.

"Ok, stay right there," Billy said crouching to look at her eye to eye. "Do you understand?" Norah nodded slowly, looking past him down into the depths of blackness. Billy gave her shoulder a squeeze before disappearing into the dark. Worried and alone in the hall, Norah's spine tingled. Every sound seemed amplified; every shadow held a horror; every noise was the approach of something evil.

Footfalls sounded on the stairs. Norah looked down the long empty hall. She could escape, hide somewhere. But what if he found Horo?" Frozen with one foot toward the hall, her body half-turned, she caught sight of Billy's black hair, shining against the dull abyss. Reaching the top of the stairs, he held something out to Norah. "He was just sitting there waiting. I think he scared the man away." He smiled. Feeling suddenly foolish, Norah returned the grin.

As terrified as she had been the first time, it was the second visit that brought back memories of anger. It was right after she had died. She was trying to understand what was happening, and she was staring out one of the windows, watching the snowfall. Suddenly she was no longer at the window, but back in the morgue. She could hear a muffled, heated discussion coming through the door. As they began to approach, she froze. Even with the room being well-lit, she could still see the transparent visage of the bleeding man standing in a corner, watching her. As he watched her, he held something out to her. It was Horo. She moved to take the wolf from the man. He shook his head and put a finger to his lips. The scene blurred as the door swung open. Norah backed up into a counter, and realized she was standing *in it,* so she crouched down.

Dr. Pryor's normal calm was nowhere to be seen. The odd, hunched medical examiner looked less than human as he spat angrily. "You have made both of these completely useless." He gestured to the mutilated bodies on two slabs.

It was then Norah recognized herself and Billy. "Billy," she whispered sadly.

"Quiet, ghoul!" Pryor growled, looking toward Norah's hiding place.

"Are the ghosts scaring the fearless doctor?" Winston, the ghoul medical examiner, sneered.

"There are no such things as ghosts." Pryor turned on Winston with disdain.

"Careful, doctor, I might not always be around to clean up your little messes."

"Don't threaten me, ghoul." Pryor sighed, "I can lay the entire thing on your head if need be."

"If that were to happen, I will destroy you, and all those wonderful little abominations." The argument continued back out into the hall. Norah moved silently toward Billy's body. Halfway across the room, the door slammed open. Norah stared at Winston and he stared back. He dropped his gaze, "You should go away, little ghost. There is nothing left for you here."

Norah squeaked in fright before disappearing through the wall.

"Hey! Where did you go?" It was Alex, bringing Norah back to the present and the dark, debris-filled basement.

The voice that answered was not Norah's.

Mistake

"This is not your first visit, my dear little ghost." Winston appeared out of the gloom. "And you brought a peculiar friend." Alex recoiled slightly. Winston's face looked like a wax figure that had slightly melted. His body smelled like an open sewer mixed with a paper mill. His clothes hung off the hunched pale body in tatters.

"Hello, Winston. I'm surprised you remember me." Norah moved between Winston and Alex. "There is trouble in the hospital." She shrugged, trying to pull the ghoul's attention to her and away from Alex. "We were hoping it might be safe here." Something in the shifty glances Winston made caused unease. The gnawing of thousands of tiny worms of fear began to eat at the area where her stomach had been.

"Safety from the doctor, or maybe his new friend?" Winston asked.

"Um," Alex offered, "both, I guess."

"Well, I think that will be all right." Winston smiled a sparsely toothed grin. "Please make yourselves at home."

Alex turned to Norah. He exhaled a sigh of relief. Norah's eyebrows knitted as Winston bent low. She thought she saw a tail disappear into a battered air vent grate. She then looked down at Alex who was bent over, letting the stress out and exhaustion in.

"Alex, I think I made a mistake," Norah whispered. "Something is not right." She nodded toward where Winston had been.

"I thought you trusted this guy!" Alex hissed.

"I never said that!" Norah sputtered, "I just thought since Dr. Pryor betrayed him, I assumed he would help us."

"You didn't know for sure?" Alex stared aghast, "You just, what, you just assumed?"

"What? He's…well, no," she bit her bottom lip, "Yeah, I assumed." Something caught her attention. To Alex's horror, Norah looked frightened. She began edging toward the door.

"Come on," she mouthed. "Run!" she yelled.

"Shit! Go!" Alex shouted back as the door exploded inward. Ceiling tiles came crashing down. Winston was screaming, in anger or in pain, Alex couldn't tell and didn't care. One of the old fluorescent light fixtures fell through Norah as she reached out to Alex. He tried to grasp her hand, but something was pulling him away. A spell shot over Alex's shoulder at Norah, and then fire plumed from off to the side. "Go!" Alex shouted again. Norah's fingers were just inches from his; she was almost to him. "No!" he shouted, pulling his hand away.

Another spell exploded near her head. Norah fought the urge to run, torn between terror and wanting desperately to help Alex. A spray of blood splashed through her. It burned as it passed, sizzling on the wall, bending her over double in pain. In the few seconds that passed, Alex was pulled further from her reach. Cursing through tears of anger and frustration, she flew up through the floors. On the third floor, she crumpled into sobs.

Alex's feet left the ground as his body went rigid. Slowly turning over and spinning, he could only see directly in front of him. He couldn't see what happened to Norah. The surrounding chaos was muted, and no debris reached his flesh even as the walls splintered around him. Finally, Alex stopped his stomach-churning movements. Upside down, he could see who had decided to torment him. The name fell from his lips like poison. "Simon."

Welcome

"I know we are not paying attention to these pathetic attempts to scare us." Aaron started walking backward in front of Chloe. "I mean, I am not worried, but—" he continued, as Chloe didn't slow her advance. "Maybe we should, I don't know, maybe add a bit of caution to our advance. Chloe's eyes went wide, her hands shot out grabbing Aaron before he could take another step. Hey, what's wrong?"

Lying on the floor in a dried pool of blood was the body of Linda. "I knew she would be here," Chloe sighed, "but it still doesn't make it any easier to see."

***

Linda woke with a start. She was lying on a dusty rug staring up at the ceiling. Realizing she was alone, her anger blossomed. "Mike! Where the hell are you?" she screamed, in self-important rage. Pushing herself up, she glared around for any sign of her companion. Gaining her feet, she suddenly realized she had left something behind. She stood still, not wanting to look back. Terrified, she dared not look at her hands, knowing what she would see. "Okay, so… this can't be happening. I am asleep, and in a minute, I will wake up and call that no good son of…" Her rant was immediately cut off by a screech escaping her throat when she held her hands close to her eyes. Slamming her eyes shut, she tried to calm the heartbeat she realized she couldn't feel. Slowly, hesitantly, she opened her eyes as she turned. Keeping her eyes above shoulder height, she held her breath. Taking a full minute, she looked at the peeling paint and filthy windows before letting her eyes fall upon her body. Her scream echoed through the empty halls. Linda then noticed she was not alone.

Chloe's fingers found the bridge of her nose. She groaned, rubbing at the irritation. She wanted to feel bad as she heard the cry of a new ghost. Knowing who this new apparition was, she suddenly found it oh-so-tiring.

"Oh, what new annoyance is this?" Liza muttered behind Chloe.

"Looks like they have a new addition," Aaron muttered in Chloe's ear. Plastering a huge fake smile on his face, he spoke good-naturedly, "I guess I should welcome them." He laughed uneasily. Chloe hissed her opposition, followed by a groan as Linda's face passed from frightened confusion to recognition.

"You! I remember you." Linda pointed accusingly at Chloe. "This is somehow your fault, isn't it?' Chloe's hands were raised in surrender. "Oh, I should have gone back," Linda fumed. "I should have gone back and had you exercised, you evil little bitch."

"Hey now, that is uncalled for," Aaron shouted.

Behind Chloe and Aaron, Liza closed her eyes, feeling the frustration. She tried to calmly interrupt a growing barrage of insults from Linda. Her teeth clenched as she tried to fight the growing annoyance. "That bitch better shut it soon," she grumbled, moving in between Aaron and Linda. She began to question the wisdom of this plan.

"Oh now, who the hell is this?" Linda spat, "Some new skank to try to scare me off. Well, up yours, I'm a ghost now too, so you can just fu—"

"There really is no need for such language," Aaron shouted, trying to shield Chloe's ears.

Frowning at him, Chloe pushed past Aaron. "Look, I am sorry I frightened you before, but as you can see, I am no longer a ghost."

Linda changed tactics at the speed of light. "Oh, so now you want to show off because I am a ghost and you're not. Want to show me you're not scared." Linda seethed. "Well I didn't just pop out at *you*." She jumped forward, causing Aaron and Chloe to reflexively jump back. "See, not so damn funny now, is it."

"I wasn't trying to be funny," Chloe protested.

Aaron's patience was reaching the end of its tether. Liza was too busy watching Chloe to see the balls of energy lighting up in his hands.

"Oh damn, that's right," Linda snarled, "you were being helpful. Warning us against the evil. Well, missy, I think you were the only evil in that house."

Liza saw Chloe's expression instantly change. The temperature dropped precipitously. The battered filthy windows began to vibrate. Tattered wallpaper and peeling paint began to strip off the walls. A wind began to whip around Chloe and Linda. Chloe's hair blew wildly as her eyes turned red. Linda was too far into her rant to even notice the danger she was in. Liza crept up behind Chloe, cautiously whispering something to her.

"You!" Linda pointed straight at Liza, "you can stay right the hell out of this." She shouted, sending a wave of anger through Liza. Glaring at Linda, Liza was ready to send a blast at her, but faltered. Flames seemed to surround Linda as she glared at them.

From behind Liza, a howling voice erupted from Chloe's throat, "How dare you!" The sheer force of her anger sent Linda stumbling back a step, while Liza ducked for cover.

Aaron decided to defuse the situation. Summoning his power, he threw an energy bolt toward Linda. His thinking, of course, was she would cry out. He had expected surprise, or pain, not the string of obscenities he received. His energy bolt was knocked off course, shattering an overturned planter. Along with the explosion and shattering, his ears were assaulted by her oaths of his destruction.

"Whoa, whoa, whoa," Aaron shouted, "That was not a fair assessment of my mother, and that other thing is physically impossible." Her replied shocked him. "My father never did such a thing," he thought for a moment, "well, not without a good reason, but that is none of your business." Aaron continued to find himself wrong-footed in the conversation. He could not get a word in edgewise against this ghost. "Oh, the hell with this," he cried. Lightning crackled in his hand, growing in intensity.

"Oh, hell no!" Linda screamed, "you are not throwing that glowing shit at me." Her rage flew out from her in waves, pushing him back. "You think you can kill me twice?" She elongated to glower down at him. "I," she took a step forward, "Will," Aaron retreated, "not," another step, "allow," and he threw a spell past her. Rage flew at him, pushing him further, "I said I will not allow it!" she screamed.

Chloe appeared, grabbing Aaron by the arm. Thankfully she was back to the person he knew. "I'm sorry," he shouted, as Liza grabbed his other arm. Linda had distorted into a hellish banshee. Aaron was still facing her as Chloe and Liza ran toward a set of doors. These were the doors Alex had been through. Chloe cringed as the searing waves of hate pulsed at her back. It wasn't on the level of Edgar's spite, but the memory drove her faster through the doors. Slamming them shut, Aaron screamed as Linda's glaring visage appeared in the small glass window. Liza cast a locking spell on the door. It rattled in its frame as Linda continued to insult everything from Aaron's manhood to his entire lineage.

Backing away, the three looked at each other. It was Chloe who summed it up, "Wow, just, wow." She shook out of the tension. "Let's find Alex," she said, trying to put a bit of distance between them and the door.

Aaron nodded. "And a safer way out of here. You know, maybe we just go find that maniac wizard who wants us dead."

"That does sound better than that crazy ghost," Liza agreed.

Chloe blew out a breath. She felt relief to have them with her.

Less than Ideal

"Oh, if it isn't Chloe's little pet," Simon chortled as he poked the sphere surrounding Alex. The effect was like someone banging a knuckle on a fish tank. The sound reverberating in Alex's eardrums. Simon's cackle still sounded clearly through the bubble.

Alex fought to move, struggling against his invisible bonds. All he could do was answer Simon's slight in the cruelest way he could. "Says the unwanted minion of Kerlvin." The effect was just as he hoped.

"Kerlvin, the Great Duke of hell, ha!" Simon seethed, "He will bow before me. Once it has been witnessed. Once Alistair and the good doctor finish my little project, all hell will know and revere me."

"Now, now, let's not get ahead of ourselves." Dr. Pryor appeared out of the gloom behind Simon. "Once my work is complete, there will be so many changes." Alex watched the malice skitter across the skeletal features. He knew Simon had no idea the danger he was in. Deeper in the shadows, Alistair loomed. His hands were moving in rhythmic patterns as he chanted something unheard.

Alex fell and his shoulders collided painfully onto the floor. Luckily, his head bounced on some fallen ceiling tiles that were wet, moldy, and squishy. Above him, Simon squealed in terror and anger. Alex couldn't help his smirk as he saw the portly demon enclosed in the same kind of bubble he had just fallen from. Simon struggled in the sphere as Alex struggled to gain his feet. His shoes found no purchase as his lungs protested the smoke and dust. The word *asbestos* flitted through his mind before powerful, clawed hands lifted him. Alex was set upright, to find struggling only brought pain. Sharp, ragged claws dug painfully into his upper arms. Alex cried out from the intense grip.

Dr. Pryor ignored his agony as he turned on his heel to become the leader of the grizzly parade. The emaciated living dead doctor was followed by a floating demon. Simon shouted curses as he sent spell after spell against the shield. Not a sound escaped nor was a dent made through the globe. A grim-faced Alistair followed, still chanting and moving his hands rhythmically. He seemed to have to concentrate to hold Simon at bay. Next was Alex. He was forced forward by the hairy clawed hands. He was aware there were other creatures, but he could not turn to see them.

"You don't have to help them," Alex called to the creature holding him and the ones that followed. It was something about the way they moved. Alex was positive these beings did not want to be slaves for Pryor. He was sure that is what they were. "My friends are coming, and we can help you."

"Be quiet," growled a rough voice.

"We have beaten Alistair before." Alex pleaded. "Both him and Simon." He struggled to turn around. The creature gripped him tighter, but it didn't use its claws. Alex took this as a good sign. "The doctor doesn't look like it would take much to take him down." Out of the corner of his eye, Alex caught a glimpse of Norah. She was holding a finger against her lips in warning. Alex shook his head. "I have another friend who can—" Alex was not able to explain what his other friend could do. They had reached a set of stairs. The next thing he saw were stars, then nothing at all.

He had no idea how much time had passed when he finally awoke. The first thing he realized was that his arms no longer hurt. The issue now was he could no longer move either of them. Alex's trouble did not stop at his arms; his legs were also immobile. He was seated and bound, that much he knew. He tried several times to open his eyes. Each time resulted in pain from the blinding white light. Muffled curses floated across the room he could not see.

"Oh my, I can see how this would be extremely infuriating." Pryor's voice took on an understanding tone.

The harsh light had gone out. Blinking in the softer light from a lamp off to the side, Alex surveyed the room. He was, indeed, strapped to a hard, wooden chair. The wood was heavily scarred and stained. Alex's stomach tightened in foreboding. Across the room, Simon's reddish-gold eyes glared at him. The demon was also strapped onto a chair that was similar to Alex's. A leather strap held Simon's head in place while braided cords held his arms fast. Another difference Alex could see were sigils burned into the wood of Simon's chair.

Pryor looked at Alex, then at Simon. Smiling, he explained, "Those funny symbols will make sure our little demon behaves." A sickening thrill ran through Alex's chest. Sticking out from the demon's spindly arm was a needle attached to a tube. Following the tube down, Alex saw an old glass IV bottle slowly filling with black blood.

Eyes wide, Alex looked down at his own arm. A similar needle and tubing were attached to a vein. While Simon's bottle was low, Alex's was hung high. Simon was being bled while Alex was getting a transfusion. Next to Simon was a glass bottle filled with red fluid, what Alex could only assume was his blood. It did not seem to be attached to Simon yet.

"This is a first." Pryor's voice held a hint of excitement.

"Again, I must protest this course of action," Alistair interrupted.

"No, no, no, this is the best result I have ever achieved from any of these creatures!" Pryor was moving closer, inspecting Alex. "I've done experiments on all sorts—wolves, bears, cats, and even sheep. This has been the best out of all." Alex recoiled from the doctor and his red splattered lab coat and smell of death. "Watch, just watch," Pryor entreated, pulling a large cleaver from a cart Alex hadn't noticed until then. It was covered in gleaming knives and other nasty looking implements.

Smiling at the sharp edge, Pryor approached Alex, who reacted to the danger. "Hey, wait. What the hell are you going to do with that?" Twisting and pulling at the strap holding his arm in place, he screamed in fright. The cleaver fell. Alex howled in agony. His hand was completely separated from his arm. Pryor moved the severed hand a few inches away from the bleeding stump.

Eyes bulging and mouth screaming, Alex could only stare as tendrils of red and black blood crept out of both his arm and the severed hand. The tendrils entwined and knitted together as he watched, fascinated. The agony he had felt turned to burning, as if his severed hand was on fire. When the process was complete, it left no evidence of the violence that had just happened to him, not the slightest trace. Eyes still wide but no longer screaming, Alex wiggled the fingers of his freshly re-attached hand.

"You fools!" Simon shouted, "You have no idea what you are dealing with!" Pryor ignored the demon. Alistair looked back and forth between Simon and Alex. His face held worry.

"I hate to admit it, but I think the demon might be right." Alistair shrugged, "I'm going to agree with the wretched little demon. This is not a good idea."

"Um, thank you?" Simon growled through gritted teeth. The look in his eyes could have burned flesh, Alex felt. "What you are doing will only end in catastrophe."

"The hell beast may be right. No one has ever done anything like this." Alistair drew in a breath. "I thought you wanted the girl, the one I told you about. She was dead, but became corporeal again."

"You leave Chloe alone!" Alex struggled against his bonds.

"Quiet!" Pryor calmly called. "She will be an interesting experiment as well, but this…" He looked lovingly at Simon, "This is an actual demon." The affection in his eyes was not dulled by Simon's spitted curses. "I never thought these creatures actually existed."

"Who do you think created all those monsters you experimented on?" Alistair gaped.

"You know nothing, stupid wizard. We did not make those, fool." Simon laughed nastily.

Alistair glared at him. "I was able to trick *you*."

Simon's smile evaporated. "For which you will pay dearly."

"Forgive me for not being frightened of a bound, helpless demon."

Alex watched the exchange in disgust. They had cut off his hand. While he was happy it had reattached, his preference would have been not had it cut off in the first place. They were playing with him and he did not appreciate it. His anger joined with one that wasn't his own. Rage began to course through his veins, carried like lightning in his demon blood.

"You should be frightened," Simon continued the bickering, "For you have no idea what you have wrought."

Both Alistair and Pryor's attention were firmly focused on Simon, who had lowered his voice dramatically.

Through a red haze, Alex watched the taunting with growing fury. Alex's eyes darted to Pryor, who seemed to sense danger. "Oh dear, we can't have that!" Pryor rushed forward. There was a glint of metal in the light. Alex felt a pinch in his arm. The room lost focus, then dissolved to black. The last thing he thought he saw was Norah's face in the wall.

Alliance

"How are we going to find Alex? This place is huge," Aaron questioned, staring at a map on the back of a door. It showed the quickest escape route. "If you say split up, I'm slapping someone," Aaron said over his shoulder, while mentally making a note of the escape route.

"If Kerlvin were here, I'd say you and Scooby check the basement while Daphne and I look upstairs," Chloe joked through her worry.

"Does that make you Fred?" Aaron asked.

"Velma, duh." Chloe laughed as she motioned for them to follow.

"I am so happy you left me out of that insipid cartoon conversation," Liza muttered.

"Hey Chloe, I think someone is feeling left out."

"She can be Fred," Chloe smirked, "or Scooby Dee." She bolted up the last few stairs and out into a hall.

"Wait," Liza paused. "Did she just call me a dog?" Aaron bit back a laugh. While Liza glared at him, he turned and ran after Chloe.

"I think Liza may kill you before Alistair gets a chance," Aaron laughed. Immediately the mirth disappeared. Before Liza could begin to tell Chloe off, she stopped. Chloe was holding up a single finger near her waist.

"Someone is here," Chloe breathed. Aaron and Liza moved like soldiers, covering Chloe from the flanks and behind. She moved slowly along the corridor. Chloe's eyes were closed as she felt and listened to the air. Stepping back from the wall, she stopped and waited. Slowly a face emerged from the peeling white paint. Chloe recognized it at once. It was the girl from the video, the one that had been with Alex.

Stepping out of the wall, Norah extended a hand. "You must be Chloe." Her tone lacked emotion or enthusiasm. Taken aback, Chloe stared at the ghost. Shaking out of her shock, she took Norah's hand.

"Pleasure to meet you, too," she replied, without being able to keep the annoyance from her voice. Her grip on the ghost tightened. "Where's Alex?" she demanded, looking over Norah's shoulder as if Alex might pop out of the wall next.

Norah pulled her hand free. "Um yeah, Alex, about him." Though she was floating several inches above the floor, Norah shuffled her feet uncomfortably.

"Oh my god," Chloe whispered. Her hands came slowly up to cover her mouth. Aaron gasped, and Liza laid a hand on Chloe's shoulder as she pulled Aaron into a one-armed hug.

"NO! Hey! Wait," Norah protested, terrified, "I think he is still alive. I mean, he was the last time I saw him, and that was only an hour or so ago." Norah cocked her head as she stared off into the distance, "Well, unless…, but no…"

Silence descended until Chloe couldn't stand it any longer. Roughly grabbing Norah by the shoulders, Chloe shook the young ghost, "Unless? Unless what!"

Pushing Chloe away, Norah rubbed her arms. "Damn, what is with you two?"sShe grumbled, "Both you and Alex are so damned handsy." She looked up to see the look on Chloe's face that demanded a quick explanation. "No, I mean, you two can touch me. It's just weird."

"And?!" Chloe demanded.

"No, no, no, he has been a perfect gentleman." Norah stepped back, shocked by Chloe's glare.

Shaking her head in frustration, Chloe growled, "Where is he?" Frowning, she continued, "Listen, I'm sorry, I trust him, and I want to thank you for looking after him, but I need to know where he is."

"Um, right, about that." Norah bit her lower lip. "We got separated." Her face crumpled, "Okay, we got betrayed by a ghoul that I thought we could trust because he and Dr. Pryor had a past. Well, I guess they got over it because it gave us up to Pryor. Winston, the ghoul, he gave us up. So then Pryor shows up with that wizard that Alex has been hiding from. Well, the next thing we know everything starts blowing up." Norah had started slow, but before Chloe could ask a single question, Norah had reached top speed. Looking apologetically at Chloe, she said, "I tried to get to him, you know, to fly him out of there, but he wouldn't let me." She looked away, not able to meet Chloe's wide-eyed stare, "I hid as Alex got taken away and…" She paused, her face tense.

Fear began to eat at Chloe's stomach. "What aren't you telling me?"

"I had a pretty good idea where they were taking him, so I went to see if I could help." Again Norah paused, shifting uneasily.

The tension built as Norah continued to shuffle her feet. Finally, it broke as all three shouted as one. "And?!!!"

"I just can't…, well I'm not sure you're even going to believe me."

"*Tell* us!" they shouted.

Norah said, "Okay, but you're going to think I'm crazy." She caught the look on Liza's face that told her it was too late on that count. Sighing Norah continued, "I went to the lab, thinking that is where they would take him while they waited for you." She gestured to Chloe, "They didn't have to wait, because…" she swallowed nervously, "they… I have no idea *how*. I didn't think they actually existed. I thought Alex was just messing with me when he said he knew one." She saw their glares, "Okay! They had a *demon*. Somehow they had captured a demon." Norah waited for them to laugh.

Instead, Chloe turned to her companions. "Kerlvin," Aaron spat before Chloe could speak. "Serves that little bastard right, but what the hell are they doing with Alex?"

He turned to Norah, who screamed as a fire erupted from the floor, along with the stench of death and sulfur.

"Those are not very nice things to call me," Kerlvin pouted.

"That's… that's a… that's a fricken' *demon*!" Norah pointed as Kerlvin wrapped his wings around himself like a cape.

"I see your choice in friends continues to be of the highest intelligence." Kerlvin smiled as he bowed to Norah, who was trying to discretely ease back into the wall. Chloe caught her by the arm.

"No, thank you," Norah protested, "I don't want anything to do with demons."

Kerlvin's claws clicked on the tiled floor as he approached Norah. She struggled in Chloe's grip but could not escape. "Hmm," he rubbed his chin as he inspected Norah, "Interesting." He gloated, "I am guessing they don't know." His smile was unsettling, to say the least.

Defeated, Norah allowed herself to be pulled back into the room.

"What did you do?" Chloe demanded.

"Nothing!" Norah shot back, anger flaring, "Alex was my friend."

"What do you mean *was*?" Chloe shouted.

"*Is*. I hope." Norah was in Chloe's face. "I was protecting him."

Suddenly Kerlvin pushed the two women apart as he continued to circle Norah. "I wasn't aware your kind could even become ghosts. Interesting." Kerlvin rubbed at his chin again.

"Your kind?" Aaron asked, confused.

Liza stood silently, her eyes closed as she held out a hand to feel the air. Cocking her head to the side, Liza spoke. "She's not human; well, not entirely."

"I'm a lycanthrope," Norah stated proudly.

Aaron thought for a moment, then eyes wide, he asked, "So you're a werewolf?"

Liza cringed while Norah looked angry and disgusted.

"Nice to see speciesism is still rampant after all these years." Norah glared at Aaron, who looked back and forth between Norah and Liz. His confusion was almost comical. Chloe had to choke back a laugh while Kerlvin rolled his eyes at Aaron's gaff.

"Werewolf is not an acceptable term," Liza whispered to him.

"Ooooh," he nodded. "Right, um, sorry about that."

Now it was Chloe's turn to roll her eyes. Aaron's brow creased, "So wait, you're dead, so you are a ghost of a were, I mean um, lycanthrope, so, can you still change into a wolf?"

Liza gasped as she shook her head. Chloe pushed past Aaron, glaring at him. "Always so considerate." She growled, turning to Norah, "Sorry about that, he's an idiot."

Norah laughed, slightly relieved and relaxing a bit.

"Oh, how nice," Kerlvin interrupted. "Here we are learning new things and growing as people. Thing is, we actually have a really big problem we need to discuss."

Chloe frowned at the demon, "Wait, if you are here, then who was the demon they had?"

"That would be Simon," Kerlvin spat, as if the name tasted nasty.

"Do you know where Alex is?" Chloe looked between Norah and Kerlvin.

"Yes, I believe we both know," Kerlvin nodded to Norah. "That is not the problem now. It is easy to know where he is. The problem is…" he hesitated.

Chloe backed up a step. Was this concern or fear on the demon's face?

Kerlvin looked directly at Chloe, "I don't know what Alex has become."

In the Blood

Alex felt the coarse leather straps tight across his forearms. He knew where he was, could hear the movement around him. He needed to know what was going on. Fighting to remain conscious, he tried opening his eyes, but his eyelids were so heavy. The darkness closed back in.

Noises of shuffling feet and the fetid smell of a filthy animal assaulted his nose. Alex felt the presence of something large moving slowly toward him. The closer it got, the more the animal smell mixed with the scent of something long dead. Suppressing a wave of nausea, Alex cracked an eye open. Through the sliver of vision, he saw something large and hairy lumber close. Then, it was out of sight. Suddenly, its distorted face swam into view again. Animal eyes peered into Alex's wide human eyes. Its horrid breath assaulted Alex's senses. The creature's bearlike face moved close., Alex tried not to cower. The beast's coarse hair brushed harshly across Alex's cheek. It hot humid breath was in his ear.

"Run. Fight." The creature grunted as the strap tight against Alex's right arm loosened. The door opened. It grunted, then moved quickly away.

Alex pretended to still be asleep. Peeking through the smallest gap in his eyelids, he watched the hairy creature lumber away. It looked to be part man and part bear, like something caught half transformed between the two. Alex felt a twinge in his chest as he gazed upon new and old lash marks on the retreating bear-man.

As the beast moved past, Alex could see Simon. He was still tightly bound, apparently still asleep. Black blood still dripped into an IV bottle through the tube still attached to the demon's arm. Alex clenched his fist as a fit of anger flowed through him. The sensation of the leather strap loosening as his muscle flexed brought Alex back to himself.

As carefully and quietly as he could, Alex continued to work his arm free. The clasp fell open as Dr. Pryor and Alistair entered the room. They were still having a heated conversation.

"The girl you seek is here, so why don't you go fulfill your petty revenge?" Pryor suggested as if he was exhausted.

"I will have my revenge and I will leave this place," Alistair growled. "I suggest you dispense with this mad idea and kill them both, immediately."

Alistair swept from the room before Pryor could answer. Alex realized he had been paying too much attention to their conversation and not enough to his escape. He pulled his hand free as Pryor turned to face him.

Time stopped as they stared at each other. Simon's laugh broke the tension. Dr. Pryor rushed toward the tray holding the syringe. Trying to pull his other arm free, Alex shouted in panic, "NO!"

A wave pulsed through the room. The doctor was thrown across the room. Simon's chair flew back and tipped over. Pryor tried to regain his footing. Alex threw out his hand, sending Pryor sprawling again. He hit the wall with a sickening crunch, to crumple at the bottom of Simon's smashed chair.

Shocked, Alex gawked at the scene. Pryor groaned. Alex wasted no time pulling at the remaining restraints. He was free. Taking a step toward the door, Alex froze. The sound of flat slapping feet moving quickly across the floor told him he had an additional problem. Simon was free.

"Get back here with my blood, you insignificant human!" Simon shouted.

Alex bounced off the doorframe as he ran. He swore as the long doorless hall stretched before him. The slapping feet were getting closer. Alex was running. A T intersection loomed ever closer. Right or left, he had to make the choice. Fire exploded to his right, sending him to the left and making the decision for him. Skidding around the corner, Alex smashed painfully into someone who let out a familiar squeak.

Reunion

Alex was laying on something smaller than he was and softer. Pushing himself up, he looked down at the most beautiful face he had ever seen. "Chloe," he breathed.

Looking back up at him with the widest smile, tears brimming in her bright blue eyes, was his Chloe. Without a word, her arms enveloped him.

"Great to see you, but is this really the time?" Liza questioned as she pulled Alex to his feet. Simon slapped around the corner and skidded to a halt.

"Oh, this is too good. I get to kill you and all your little friends." Simon grinned.

His cackle turned into a gurgle. Kerlvin appeared from behind Liza. Norah's ghostly face watched as the two demons eyed each other. Simon looked wary, while Kerlvin appeared resolute.

"Well, if it isn't my wayward minion." Kerlvin's black claws clicked together menacingly.

"I have no master, and I will never be your subject," Simon shouted, sending a blur of spells at Kerlvin.

Lightning crackled along the wall, sending razor-sharp shards of tile raining down on Chloe and her friends.

Chloe swore and pointed past the dueling demons. Alistair had appeared behind Simon. Liza fired a spell at him. Alistair returned it in kind. Norah motioned for everyone to follow. Aaron tried pulling Alex and Chloe.

Alex's anger burned red hot through his veins. He threw a wave down the hall. His aim, not the best, sent Kerlvin into Simon, while Alistair was blown back into the gloom. Silence filled the hall as everyone stared at Alex.

Dr. Pryor turned the corner, surveying the damage. "This is a most interesting development," he said calmly.

Chloe pushed past Alex to glare at the doctor. "What did you do to him?"

"Is this the creature you were waiting for?" Pryor inquired doubtfully to Alistair, who limped back into view.

"Don't be fooled, she is not what she appears," Alistair protested.

"She is nothing but a little girl," Pryor chuckled.

The walls seemed to bow outward from Chloe. "Little girl?" she growled. "You hurt Alex." She stepped closer. Her eyes turned black as her face grew gaunt. "You threatened ghosts." Another step, and a green haze flowed from her hands as her fingers grew longer and her nails turned black and claw-like.

Liza was now pulling Alex and Aaron back. Norah watched in terrified transfixion. As everyone watched, Kerlvin took the opportunity to strike at Simon.

The hall exploded. Plaster and tile rained down. Pryor ducked and ran. Alex was knocked down by the number of explosions and magic flying back and forth. Sitting up, he coughed through the dust that was covering him and still falling. As he brushed the dust from his hair and clothes, he watched Liza storm past him, her growl turned to a furious cry.

Suddenly a wall disappeared in an explosion of fire and lightning. Aaron fell back, knocking heavily into Chloe, who barely kept her footing. Then she fell back onto Alex. She had returned to her normal self.

"This is not the place for this," Chloe shouted, shielding her head from falling debris.

"This way," Norah called.

"That is a wall. Unlike you, we can't go through a wall," Aaron screamed over another hail of spells.

"It is a secret door! Come on!" Norah beckoned.

"Liza, come on!" Aaron called from the entry of the secret door.

She turned to his voice. Chloe watched Liza throw a spell and run toward her. Blue flame filled the hall along with screams. Liza was running when the hallway began to collapse.

Goodbye

The first thing Chloe became aware of was a dull ache in the back of her skull. Through her daze, she could make out Alex coughing somewhere close. She could feel his body shudder next to hers, even though the sound was reaching her as if coming from far away. As she tried to discern his proximity, another sound she could not define caught her ear. It was like the old radio her father had in the living room, that only he could tune in. It sounded like a poorly received signal fading in and out, just like the focus of her eyes. It was a voice and it was panicked, bordering on hysterical.

Her vision improved slightly. She could tell now that it was smoke and dust that filled the air, obscuring her sight.

Alex's face swam into view. "Chloe, Chloe, Chlo, are you okay?" He was inches from her face, but still sounded far off.

She nodded, instantly regretting it as the dull ache turned into a spike running through her brain. Closing her eyes from the pain, she let the sensation subside. Alex had left her side. She could feel his absence. Something terrible had to have happened, for him to leave her at a time like this.

Opening her eyes, Chloe saw Alex through the chaos. He was crawling toward a kneeling figure. Slowly her double vision combined to reveal Aaron. He was frantic. His eyes were searching everywhere as he screamed for help. A horrid feeling began to descend into the pit of her stomach. Pushing herself up on to her elbows, nausea threatened to overtake her. Fighting through it, she turned over and began to crawl. She had to get to the person lying unmoving on the floor. She had to see for herself. It couldn't be true.

No, no, no, no, repeatedly crashed through her mind. Then for a glorious moment, she relaxed. Everything was fine. Liza was standing there, not a scratch on her. Then Chloe realized Liza was looking *down* at Aaron. Liza's face, at first, held confusion. As if sensing Chloe watching, Liza raised her eyes to meet Chloe's. It was then the confusion slowly morphed into comprehension, then anger.

Chloe was on her feet without realizing when it happened. Slowly, Liza and Chloe advanced toward each other. Liza began to speak as she approached. "I survived witch hunters, rebellions, the Inquisition, and the Nazis," she fumed. "This is how I die!?" she demanded, pointing to her body.

"I am so, so, sorry," Chloe whispered. Tears began to roll down her cheeks. Seeing her friend's anguish, Liza's anger evaporated.

"I didn't want to go either," Chloe whispered. "I was in that well all night. I don't know how long I would have lasted if…" Chloe couldn't finish; she shuddered at the memory. Liza pulled her close, comforting her friend.

"Oh, sweetheart," she whispered, slowly wiping a tear from Chloe's cheek.

"Other than this," she gestured to the scene behind her, "the last couple of years have been some of the best."

Looking past Liza, Chloe saw Aaron. His pain tore through her heart, adding to her sorrow.

Seeing where she was looking, Liza turned her gaze to Aaron. Grabbing Chloe by the shoulders, she demanded her attention. "Fear is yours now. I can't trust Aaron to take him on." Forcing herself to look back to Aaron, Liza straightened up. Aaron was clinging to Alex, begging him to help, to do something. "I don't want to leave him," Liza whispered, turning back to face Chloe.

The two friends wore mirrored expressions of pain. Suddenly, something lit up Liza's face. "You will always be my sister," she said, pulling Chloe close.

Smiling, Chloe replied, "And you will always be mine."

"Tell Alex," Liza smirked, "he is lucky he got someone so out of his league." She kissed Chloe on the cheek before gliding toward Aaron. "Tell Alex it is okay. I have something I want to give Aaron."

The Promise

Chloe wrapped her arms around Alex's shoulders. "Shhh," she whispered in his ear as Aaron suddenly went rigid.

Aaron was on top of a mountain. Green grass and grey stone surrounded him in every direction. "Oh, how I have missed the highlands," Liza sighed. Her hand held his arm while her head lay on his shoulder. Aaron shifted to hold her in an embrace.

"Do you have to go?" his voice cracked as he asked.

"Aye, my love, I am sorry, but I do."

"Why?" His eyes pleaded with her not to go.

"Oh, my sweet bonnie lad, do you not understand?" She stroked his cheek, "I have lived for so long. Magic keeps me looking young, but I am so old now."

"I don't care." Aaron stated angrily, "I don't, and I can't let you leave me."

"I'm sorry, my love, but I do not have a choice."

"Chloe didn't leave," he argued.

"Dearest, please."

"I know, I know, it just hurts so much," he conceded.

"I will always be a part of you," she said, and she smiled.

"People always say that." He pulled her close as tears began to fall.

"Oh, aye, they do," she embraced him tighter, "but I mean it literally." Light erupted around them as Liza's body slowly entered his.

***

Aaron was shaking and shuddering, and light was shooting from his fingertips. Alex gasped as he tried to pull free from Chloe. "What's going on?"

"It's okay," Chloe calmed him, "she is giving him her magic and a promise."

Alex spun to face her. "What the hell does that even mean?"

"It means," she replied calmly, "she'll be there for him when he needs her." The light faded from around Aaron. He slumped over Liza's broken body. Her head and shoulders lay in his lap, while her chest lay crushed under a concrete support. She had been a whirlwind of magic and swearing only moments ago. Aaron looked into the face he had come to know could overcome anything. Her expression was calm, at peace.

"She's home," Aaron stated as he laid her head on the floor. Looking up, he said, "Come on, we can't stay here."

Gaining his feet, Alex spied Norah watching them from halfway into a wall. "Tell Winston she is off limits!"

Norah nodded. "I really don't think he survived the morgue." She shrugged.

"Even better," Alex growled.

Welcome Battle

Aaron burst through the doors and ran upstairs before Alex and Chloe could stop him. In a blink, they lost sight of him. Gasping, Alex waved toward the last direction they had seen him go. "No, keep going, we're just," his voice rising to a shout, "fine back here!" Chloe frowned at him, but did not debate the fact they had lost track of Aaron. Norah glided after Aaron. She poked out of walls or doors, helping to guide them. Finally catching up, they found a frustrated Aaron stomping back and forth, trying to decide which way to go next.

"Oh, are my little rats lost in the maze?" Alistair's voice echoed through the hall. Aaron did not look up as he gave the speaker the finger. Chloe sighed, as if the taunts were not worth her time.

Alex paused to brush the years from an old floor map on the wall. "If I am reading this right, we are only a floor below the long term ward," Alex explained.

Chloe was already on the third step by the time the rest started to follow. Aaron, grumbling, brought up the rear. Chloe's hand rested on the door handle when the speaker crackled into life again.

"Through that door awaits some of my friends," Alistair laughed. "They are looking forward to eating, oh, I mean *meeting*, you."

"I think that was lame even back in my day," Chloe sighed. "And you used that already!" she shouted at the speaker.

Without hesitation, she turned the knob and was through the door. Alex jumped past her, ready for a fight. Aaron slipped in, lightning crackling in his hands. But the hall was empty, except for the faint glow of Norah and the lightning from Aaron.

"Well, that was anti-climactic," Chloe muttered. The tension dissipated.

"We aren't talking about nights with my brother," Aaron joked, earning him a glower from Chloe and a smack from Alex. Aaron seemed to be waiting for something else. The realization crept slowly across his face. Liza was not there to chastise him. Sadness crashed over him, taking his breath away. Bent over hands on his knees, Aaron let a sob wrack his body. Norah laid a ghostly hand on his back. To her disappointment, it went through.

"I wish I could help," Norah whispered. The pain was in her voice. "The best I can tell you is, at least she is not here." She looked helplessly at Chloe. "She moved on."

"I know. 'Don't pity the dead' and all of that." Aaron stood, swiping at his eyes. "It just hurts so much."

Static accosted their ears, followed by Alistair's mocking tone. "Oh, do we miss our dearly departed?"

Alex pulled back on Aaron's arm. Destroying the speaker would not help them find Alistair.

"Norah," Chloe whispered, as Aaron planned the death Alistair was about to receive, "Where can he be, to use the intercom?" Norah looked around, as if the answer would pop out of the woodwork.

"Any nurse's station, or the main security office. Those are the only places I know." Norah shrugged, feeling useless. Then she heard it, and by the looks they were exchanging, her companions heard it too. The sound of clumsy shuffling noises came from further down the hall. Shadows danced through the dim light, spilling through several open doors. Fire returned to Aaron's hands. Alex resumed his stance, ready for a fight. With a nod of understanding, Chloe readied a gurney to send flying. The flames from Aaron's hands added to the shadow pattern on the wall. A noise Alex had heard before filled the hall. He knew it from old failed video games and a smattering of times when things didn't go the way someone wanted them to.

"Awww, maaan!" Disappointment drew out the words. Aaron's shoulders slumped as the undead shuffled out form the darkness. "Zombies, really? Zombies? That is *so* 2005."

Turning his back on the approaching creatures, he glared at Chloe, as if it were her fault. "Who still thinks zombies are scary? I mean…" he grabbed an old IV stand and walked up to the closest ghoul, "everyone knows how to kill them." Alex watched in terror as the zombie's hands clawed at Aaron's sleeve. Aaron, annoyance written across his face, batted the hand away. "Seriously, you just—" he thrust the sharp metal end through the creature's eye socket. A squelching crunch caused Chloe to regret eating before they arrived. Norah's face held a look usually reserved for something stuck to your shoe. "Destroy the brain, and voilà!" He pulled the stand free. Quickly stepping back, he avoided the collapsing zombie.

For the next five minutes Alex, Chloe, and Norah watched as Aaron worked out his anger and frustration. It was also mixed with a strange joy. "I think one of his fondest dreams is coming true." Alex watched his brother smash a skull, then spin to shove a broken chair leg up through a chin into the brain of another undead.

"You know, this is even better than a first-person shooter," Aaron yelled back, "You really feel the crunch when it goes through the skull."

Alex and Chloe turned with wide eyes as Norah stated, disgusted, "That is sick." She became aware of them staring at her. "What? You kill these creatures for fun?"

Alex stuttered, confused. "What? No. It's not real. It's just a video game." He could tell this made very little sense to someone who died in the fifties. "I'll explain later."

"Hey, that was awesome. What are you guys talking about?" Aaron asked, a huge smile and zombie gore plastered on his face.

"Idiot." Alex shook his head at his brother. Chloe nodded as she passed.

"What?" Aaron demanded.

Norah glided past, glaring, a look of confused disgust scrunched up her face.

"What?!" Aaron shouted as he followed.

They had barely made it past the rooms where the zombies had come from when their progress halted again. This time it was caused by low growling and clicking claws on the tile.

Chloe took a stumbling step back as a large snout appeared, sniffing around an open door. "Rats," she yelped. "I do not like rats." Chloe swiped a hand through the air. The gurney from the end of the hall flew past her, smashing into the hairy body that emerged from the room. It lay motionless, pinned to the wall. Before she could relax, about twenty more spilled out into the hall. Overcome in disgust, Chloe fell back.

Alex pulled her away as Aaron took up the attack. Chloe's look of disgust was now due to the stench of burnt fur and sizzling rat meat. Alex pummeled several of the creatures while Aaron burned them. Chloe sent whatever she could at the creatures. She really hated Alistair.

The lone surviving rat writhed in agony as Aaron continued to send lightning through it, until "POP!" Entrails and gore splattered the walls. "Oh man, that was awesome!" Aaron shouted.

"Not sure what is more disgusting." Chloe stuck out her tongue.

"The dead rats or his glee?" Alex finished her thought. They both laughed, then gagged on the smell.

In the old security office, Alistair stared dumbfounded at the monitors. "How?" he demanded. "Not one of them died!"

"Maybe your power is not as grand as you first expected," Kerlvin replied. He spun slowly in the squeaking chair, holding the still-cursing head of Simon. Alistair recoiled as black blood and entrails dripped from Simon's severed spine, which dangled down from his severed head.

"How are you even here?" Alistair demanded, a blue flame erupting in his hand. "I thought I destroyed you both, along with the witch."

"That is neither here nor there. What you should think about is coming quietly," Kerlvin replied, unconcerned. "You've made several terrible mistakes." Simon spat blood and oaths of destruction as Kerlvin spoke calmly. "Killing the young warlock's love was only the most recent. Oh, and it was a terrible idea—" the demon scratched his chin with his free claws, "allowing this pitiful fool's blood to be given to Alex. Oh, shut up." Kerlvin lost patience with Simon's threats. Sulfur and fire erupted in his hand, consuming Simon's screaming head. Shaking a few remaining strands of wiry black hair from his fingers, he addressed Alistair. "You have created an enemy far more dangerous than you can imagine." Kerlvin's wings extended as his tail shot out like a whip. "So, I make the offer to come with me to hell and avoid the agony. Well, no, you will still be in agony, but at least your death will be quick."

"Never!" The security office filled with blinding blue light. When it subsided, the old chair was a twisted, melted chunk of burnt metal. Alistair's breathing sounded like he had run a mile. He smiled, satisfied—until he heard Kerlvin's laugh.

"You do realize you chose poorly in this arena, do you not?" Kerlvin asked, from right beside Alistair. The wizard started, sending energy streaking across the wall. "You did not even think there might be something far, far worse than you here." Kerlvin's tongue flicked across his lips. "This will be fun." In a blast of flame, the demon disappeared.

Furious, Alistair sent oaths of violence after the thinning smoke. Fuming, he returned his attention to the security screens. Slamming his fist against the ancient console, he howled in frustration. If his attention had been on the lower monitor, he might have seen something lumbering along the hall. He might have noticed it was something out of a nightmare that even he would fear.

Sorrows of Saint Mary's

Chloe couldn't get the smell out of her nose. Alex showed signs of dehydration and exhaustion. The only water she could find was a moldy stagnant pool that smelled worse than the burnt rats and festering corpses. She really hated this place. Aaron's head drooped and his hands covered his face. Chloe knew another wave of sadness had taken him. Alex was almost asleep, but his breathing was far too rapid. When Chloe turned to ask Norah if she knew of any clean water, what she saw shocked her. Norah was holding a battered stuffed wolf. She was whispering to it.

"Horo, is this all my fault?" She looked over the broken bottles and vulgar graffiti. "Like what happened to my family and Billy. Is this because of me?" She jumped, not knowing Chloe had arrived at her shoulder.

"Why would you think that?" Chloe asked.

Norah hesitated, not wanting to tell her new friends the story, but unable to keep it in any longer. "When I first started to change it was very hard on me. I started late, later than my younger sister. It was so easy for her. For me, it hurt so much. Then when I did change, I wasn't me for hours. I was more beast, more wolf." She smiled shyly as she shook Horo gently at Chloe. "My father heard about this doctor, who apparently knew about our kind and knew how to help us." Her face darkened. "It was all lies."

Norah absently rubbed at the back of her neck. "We were on our way here, and it was snowing, badly. I was feeling really unwell, not the normal change feelings; I was so hot. I opened the window even though it was so cold. I can still see my sister's face as she held Horo between her hands." Norah rubbed her neck again. Chloe moved closer to look at the spot Norah kept rubbing. "I felt a sharp pain, right here." Chloe saw a small mark on the transparent skin. "Then I started to change. I remember the screaming, and the blood from my claws." She shut her eyes tight, trying to block the memories. "When I woke up, I was here." She looked around at the litter-strewn floor. "I met Billy here. He was wonderful and kind. He was one of the orderlies and he was my friend." A light blush colored her white cheeks. "We sorta had a thing." She shrugged, and her smile fell in despair. "Dr. Pryor caught us, and," she rubbed at her neck again, "we were outside, and I changed, but I didn't attack Billy. He was saying something when I lost consciousness." She rubbed again. "I think he forced me to change."

"Billy?" Chloe asked, startled.

"No, Dr. Pryor. He wanted to experiment on me. He has been doing this for years. He finds changeling creatures and he does—" her tears fell now, "he tries to figure out how we heal. How only certain things can kill us."

"You mean like silver bullets and decapitation?"

"Silver bullets do nothing, and who wouldn't die, if their head got cut off?" Norah frowned. "No, I mean there has to be a lot of damage to kill one of us, or it might take something as common as holly. I think that is what killed my family. We ended up in a bunch of holly bushes and with their injuries, from me and the accident, they couldn't heal."

Chloe rubbed Norah's back comfortingly. "None of that was your fault. I think you're right about him forcing you to change." She didn't mention the spot on Norah's neck. "What he did was awful, and you were a victim as well." Chloe crouched to look Norah in the eye. "And Alistair has had a grudge against us for ruining his chance at power and immortality."

Norah began to cry harder. "Yes, but without me… without me getting angry," her arms spread wide as she took in the room again, "angry at the state of this place, at being trapped here, at never seeing Billy, at not ever-changing again since he," Chloe knew that "he" was the sick doctor, "did that to me, to Billy—maybe that demon was right, maybe those like us don't become ghosts and the blood he used on Billy, my blood, made it so he couldn't come back to me." She grabbed Chloe's hands in her icy grip, "He told me he would always protect me and I sent him to oblivion."

"I'm sure you didn't, just like I am sure you had nothing to do with us being here," Chloe reassured even as she wondered if her touch as a ghost had been so cold.

"No," Norah swallowed her tears, "You don't understand. The reason Alistair found this place, met with Pryor, got his demon, did what he did to Alex, and caused your friend's death, is because of me."

"How is that even remotely possible?" Chloe asked kindly. Her brow furrowed instantly, "Wait, what? What happened to Alex?"

"I'll explain once she tells her story," Alex spoke up weakly. Chloe saw that both Aaron and Alex watching and listening. "Really, I'm fine, I think." Alex waved to Norah to continue.

Trespassing

For years and years, the hospital had been full of people. Some were alive, others were not. Norah made friends and lost them over and over, until it became too painful. As times changed and years passed, the hospital fell into neglect. It was falling apart well before the police came. After the place was closed, Norah was alone with the darkness. No other spirits roamed the halls, at least not any that would show themselves. She was aware of the strange creatures lurking in the lower levels, or out on the grounds. She watched them disappear into the small building on the grounds. She had an idea of what they were. She was sure they were the failed experiments. There were bears, rabbits, deer, and even an elk, but no other wolves. So Norah never thought to follow.

It had all become so routine, so lonely. The long-empty hospital attracted a new type of visitors. These people were not the kind Norah wanted here. It was better to be alone than with them. The more that came, the more she despised them. They were desecrating her home, and she'd had enough.

Norah had stood at the top of the stairs, frowning, as beams of light danced along the walls, cutting the darkness. Hushed whispers, nervous conversations, and uncomfortable laughter rose to meet her ears. The stairwell was already heavily graffitied, the stairs covered in broken plaster and empty bottles. Norah's anger grew. She hated them. She was sick of the things they were doing, and in her home. That awful group who stuck needles in their arms and smoked that foul-smelling stuff. She found it repulsive. They were always yelling. She hated the breaking glass of bottles and windows. The teenagers stealing away for a night of pleasure were disgusting. She couldn't understand why they would come to this filthy, neglected, drafty place to do *that*. "Get out," she whispered.

A bottle smashed on the landing, followed by swearing. "What the hell, man?"

"What? I fuckin' tripped. What the hell do you care? It was my bottle."

"That means you'll want to drink mine, and I ain't got enough to get us both messed up."

"Get out," Norah growled.

The lights flew about in their bizarre dance as the sound of a struggle ensued. "Get off, ya bastard."

"Listen dumbass, I paid for this, so hand it over."

"Get out," Norah spoke.

"Whoa dude, wait. Did you hear that?"

"Whatever man, just give me a drink." The lights were stationary.

"I said, get out!" Norah's voice gained in volume as the anger flowed through every word.

"Fuck you," one of them retorted.

"Yeah, this isn't your place. We can drink wherever we want."

"You don't have to be a dick, you know. Just let us know you're screwing and we'll leave you alone."

Norah shook. The strangers, the nasty things they did to each other and to themselves, the way they treated her home, it all burned inside her. The years that had passed, the fact she was still here. She looked down at the toy in her hand. "Enough," she breathed.

"Yo, you wanna come down here and tell me to leave?" An angry voice called up from below, followed by a snicker.

"Or maybe if you are lonely, we can come up," the snickering man called.

Norah was a volcano that had been capped too long. "I SAID GET OUT!" she screamed. More broken plaster rained down. She took a step down onto the stairs, and the whole building shook. "GET OUT OF MY HOME!" She jumped to the landing. Two beams of light were pointed straight up at her, and through her. As one young man stared, the other turned, tripped, and half-fell, half-ran down the stairs.

Norah stood on the landing shaking with rage. "Get AAAAOOOOOOOOWOOOOOT," she howled. The shadow of a great wolf fell across the wall.

Tears ran down the face of the man. The front of his pants soaked through and a puddle formed at his feet. The bottle fell from his hand with a thud as he turned and ran.

A scream of terror, combined with falling and banging, grew further away.

The light still shown on the empty wall. She looked at her hands in the light. They were the same as always, small, transparent, and human. She glanced back up the stairs. Her toy wolf lay on its side, forgotten in her anger. Gliding back to it, she picked it up, inspecting it carefully. "That shadow couldn't have been you," she looked closely at the face, "because I could see the teeth, and you just have a smile."

Her howl of fury had carried. As she reached the lobby only a few vagrants remained. A couple of them were passed out drunk, while the others seemed nervous. "We're fine. Only a few left." Norah spoke to her stuffed companion. "What do you think? Should we try the same trick? No, you're right, let's just go with the howl." Staying hidden in shadow, she let loose a long mournful howl. The sound filled the room with its anger and sorrow.

Even those in a drunken stupor awoke and fled in terror. In the flickering firelight of their barrel, a magnificent giant wolf shadow graced the wall. Smiling, Norah gave the toy a hug. "See? It's okay." The shadow seemed to leap and gnash its teeth. Norah's heart sank. As she approached the wall, the shadow evaporated. She was alone again. The silence closed in around her. "They are gone," she told Horo as she sank to the floor. "They won't bother us." Sobs wracked her body as she held the wolf toy close. "You are safe."

After a while, she began to calm. "Come on." Standing, she gripped Horo tight. "Let's go back to our room, okay?" She nodded while heading back through the doors and up the stairs. "Don't let them bother you. Remember, they can't get to us. We made sure they would never want to come back here."

Next Step

"That is very interesting and all, but I don't see how that pertains to us." Aaron shrugged. Chloe balled her fists at his insensitivity. Shaking her hands out, she let it pass, as Norah explained.

"When Alistair first arrived, I saw one of the drunkards from the night I scared them away." She sighed, "He must have told Alistair about the giant wolf, and that is why he is here."

"Too bad it is just a projection and you can't actually become a giant wolf." Aaron again pointed out a painful fact.

"Nice, Aaron," Chloe growled. "Norah, this isn't your fault. Now, what did he do to *you*?" She spun on Alex, surprising him. Alex explained about being captured, and the blood transfusion experiment. Wriggling his hand and fingers, he told how the blood had healed him. Aaron inspected Alex's hand while Chloe covered her mouth in horror. "Then I, I guess I just magically pushed them and ran," Alex ended lamely.

"Do you think we can use your blood to bring Liza back?" Aaron shouted, grabbing Alex's reattached hand. Suddenly Aaron's eyes rolled up in his head. Alex, horror-stricken, shook his brother. Aaron's mouth was moving but no sound came out. An instant later, Aaron pushed Alex away. "Knock it off."

"Dude, what the hell just happened?"

"Liza told me it wouldn't work," Aaron pouted.

"Is she a—?" Alex looked around quickly.

"No, apparently she is now in here." Aaron tapped the side of his head.

"That could get awkward," Norah whispered to Chloe, who was barely able to mask her laugh as a cough.

Regaining her composure, Chloe addressed the others. "Okay, what do we know?"

"Not much, really," Alex sighed, as he laid a hand on his brother's shoulder. "We know what we lost, but we have no idea about Pryor, Alistair, Simon, or even Kerlvin."

"Not to mention the were—," Aaron shot a glance at Norah and Chloe, "I mean, um…"

"Just go with semi-human." Norah frowned.

"Right, that lot." Aaron blushed. "Alex's furry friends. We need to know whose side they are on, or what side they will take."

Norah continued to frown. Aaron looked to Chloe to see what he had done wrong this time. She could only shrug in response. Finally, Norah spoke, "I think I know where they are. There is a building on the grounds, it was called the Abbey."

"Why?" Aaron asked.

Alex groaned, "This place is called Saint Mary's."

"Yeah, and?"

"It was set up by the Catholic Church, and the nuns stayed in the building, hence?" Alex prodded.

"Oooooohhhhh." Aaron seemed to finally get it. "Please, continue." He politely inclined his head to Norah.

"Has he sustained a lot of head injuries?" Norah whispered to Chloe. Chloe's response was a shake of her head as she applied pressure to the bridge of her nose. Norah sighed before continuing. "I saw several of the semi-humans coming and going, but I have never been there."

"Interesting," Aaron scratched at his chin, "It is interesting that ghosts, who have no lungs, seem to sigh a lot."

"Ok, now you are just being an ass." Chloe pushed Aaron away. He giggled a little while protesting the humor of it.

"So, what is the problem?" As she spoke Chloe slapped her own head, "We can't get out there."

"There has to be a way around that." Alex jumped in, "I mean there were a couple of different ones when I was caught, and still a couple of others in the lab."

"So, they must either not count against the barrier or..." Aaron offered, but no one seemed to be paying attention. "Hey, seriously, it is either that or the barrier extends to the Abby. Or the third option—" they grudgingly gave him their attention, "there is a secret passage like the one Norah brought us through."

"No, there is no passage," a quiet voice spoke from the shadows. Stepping into the light was a young woman. Around her wrists and neck were shackles. On top of her head, sticking out of gray and black long hair, were two roundish animal ears. What shocked Alex the most was the swishing gray and black ringed tail. The raccoon girl kept her head down, so as to not make eye contact.

"Hello," Chloe stepped forward, hand out in greeting, "My name is…" she faltered as the girl flinched. Dropping her hand to her side, Chloe continued, "My name is Chloe. Do you know how we can contact the others," she swallowed nervously, glancing back at Norah, who shrugged, "the others like you?"

"You are a wolf." The woman pointed at Norah. "I can sense the wolf about you, but you are also," she approached, letting a hand pass through Norah's shoulder. The woman jumped back, looking at her hand. "You are also a ghost." She was sniffing around Norah now. "I've never met a ghost before." Something shifted in Norah's features. A deep guttural growl seemed to come from everywhere around them.

"Back off, raccoon," Norah grunted through clenched teeth.

Backing away but never losing sight of Norah, the woman bared sharp canines. Hissing and chattering, the raccoon's tail expanded in anger. Alex jumped between the two. "What the hell is going on with you two?"

Norah was the first to come to her senses. "Oh my god, I am so sorry." Norah shrunk back, embarrassed.

"No, no, it was completely my fault." The tail began to return to normal. "My name is Kyrie, and I want to help. Sometimes, after what Master did to us, our baser instincts come out." She smiled sheepishly at Norah. "I'm sorry, I really am. It's just that we have heard of wolves, but we have never met one."

"Most "others" like us, don't want us around." Norah shrugged.

Kyrie caught the hurt in her eyes. "At least they never called you a rodent or garbage eater." The two smiled at each other in understanding. Kyrie tilted her head to the side, "The Indian boy, Billy, he gave you that." She pointed to the stuffed wolf.

"It was my sister's."

"You can't change, can you?" Kyrie asked.

"How did you know?"

"May I see it?" Kyrie held out her hand. Norah tentatively handed over the toy. "Try to now."

Norah stared. "I haven't been able to transform since before the—" Norah stopped talking. There were gasps and a whistle of appreciation. Norah realized she was looking down on others, her head near the ceiling.

"Giant Ghost Wolf!" Aaron shouted, "Damn, you are awesome!"

Norah returned to her normal size. Kyrie handed the stuffed wolf back. "He gave you this to help you, to keep you safe." She smiled at Norah. "He must have really cared about you."

"Yes, and Pryor killed him, because of me."

"Billy was always kind. His death is one more reason I want to help you against Master."

Blame

Dr. Pryor tapped furiously at a sigil on the back of his hand. Alistair coughed and swore through the swirling dust. Heavy footfalls came from the stairwell behind Alistair. A couple of creatures that could only be called minotaurs pushed Alistair out of the way. They easily lifted heavy beams and broken concrete off their master. Pryor shook off their hands as soon as he was standing upright. Glaring, he advanced on Alistair.

Throwing up a shield of energy, Alistair stood his ground. The first minotaur threw a punch at the shield. The air was full of the flying beast and the stench of burnt flesh. The creature did not get up once it came to earth. "I don't suggest you send another one of your beasts," Alistair shouted.

"You dare try to kill me!" Pryor shouted. "I will burn you."

"I did nothing of the sort!" Alistair shot back, "If your little experiment hadn't escaped, none of this would have happ—." He ducked quickly as a huge concrete block, thrown by a minotaur, disintegrated on his shield. Alistair flung a spell at the offending beast. Its head exploded, sending blood and brains to mix with the dust and rubble. Alistair's evil grin returned. Pryor looked shocked to be covered in gore.

"Destroy him!" Pryor ordered the last minotaur to attack. The beast looked dumbly between Pryor and Alistair then back again, clearly unsure and frightened. "I said attack!" Pryor pressed hard on a sigil. The minotaur howled in anger and pain. Instead of charging at Alistair, it advanced on Pryor. "What are you doing?! I am your master." He pressed harder on the sigil. Through the obvious agony, it continued to advance.

"Need some help there, Doc?" Alistair laughed cruelly.

Pryor was edging around the minotaur's reach. Now between the beast and the wizard, he began backing toward Alistair as fast as his emaciated legs could safely carry him over the ruble.

"You know, I could easily kill you from here," Alistair pointed out. "If your friend there had half a brain, he could just gore you on those horns."

"Will you please be quiet?" Pryor tried to retain his calm tone, even though panic laced each word. "I may have been mistaken about what happened here."

"*May* have been mistaken?" Alistair rubbed at his cheek. "So, the ensuing explosion could easily have been the collision of spells?" Pryor nodded quickly. The energy from Alistair's shield began to singe his dry flesh. "You now believe some of this destruction could have been made by the feuding demons.

"Yes, yes, you were correct all along." The energy shield burned into Pryor's back for a second longer. The minotaur exploded, drenching the doctor in blood and pieces of furry meat.

The energy evaporated. Alistair stood a couple of steps away, up the stairs. He looked down on Pryor with sadistic amusement. The animosity passing between them blinded them to the scurry of small feet that disappeared into the darkness.

Alistair led the way out of the destruction. Behind his back, Pryor was busy carving a new sigil into his left forearm. If the wizard hadn't been feeling so smug, he might have been on his guard. Pryor was going to get even with him, and then he would bleed this fool dry. A thought occurred to him as they walked down the hall. Maybe magic itself would help him retain youth.

As he carved, he could feel the minotaur's blood mixing with his own. It gave him strength, a vitality he had not felt in a long time. He considered this feeling. Maybe it was like those who drank too much. As Pryor had used more and more of the creature's blood to maintain himself, the more it took. He had thought this was because the creatures were no longer pure, that their blood had been diluted. What if it was as strong as ever, and since he had stopped using the transfusions for a long time, his tolerance had lowered? A ghost of a smile played on his lips.

Alistair paused at a door. The battered impression of an "employees only" sign still could be seen through the years of neglect. "Why are we stopping here?" Pryor asked.

"You're covered in blood, meat, and filth." Alistair wrinkled his nose at the doctor. "Quite frankly, you stink." He snapped his fingers. The employee lounge became brightly lit, and a shower began running in the back of the room.

Left alone, Pryor wrung out as much blood as he could from his clothes. He made small cuts in his body, then squeezed all he could from his garments into the wounds. Once that was exhausted, he stood under the freezing water. It didn't bother him. His nerves had been deadened to pain years ago. As had his sense of taste, which was a good thing, as he tore and chewed at the chunks of minotaur meat that clung to him. When the shower ended, Pryor's skeletal frame held more muscle and color. He found some old scrubs, shook out the dust, and put them on. Smiling into the cracked mirror, he noticed his new clothes hid his revitalized body nicely.

"Oh, you foolish, foolish wizard." Pryor chuckled, approaching the door.

Ally?

"So, you are saying you can come and go through the barrier, no problem?" Chloe asked excitedly.

"Master and the wizard don't consider us humans, so the magic doesn't work on us," Kyrie said sadly. "He is right, we aren't humans, and we aren't beasts. We are in-between, unaccepted in both worlds."

"Like some kind of messed up magical Island of Doctor Moreau," Aaron exhaled. Everyone turned to stare. "What?" he demanded.

"Nothing, it is just... that was an appropriate comparison," Alex replied, as Chloe nodded approvingly behind him. Then Alex lost his balance slightly. "I'm okay," he reassured quickly, holding a hand out to keep Chloe from grabbing him.

"Um, do you have any food and water?" Chloe hesitated, "That would be safe for him?" Kyrie nodded. She pulled a small canteen from a bag slung across her chest. "Small sips, thank you," Chloe instructed Alex, as she thanked Kyrie. At first, Chloe didn't notice the small piece of what looked like bark that Kyrie held out. "What is that?" she asked finally, noticing the small quiver of the hand that held the item.

"Just a bit of jerky," Kyrie mumbled. Alex took it gratefully, ripping off a piece and chewing appreciatively.

"Um, hi, yeah," Norah nervously enter the conversation, her small arm raised, "What is our friend eating," she eyed the meat apprehensively, "exactly?"

"Squirrel jerky," Kyrie smiled shyly. Aaron looked aghast. Chloe's brows knitted at his response.

Alex, on the other hand, stopped chewing, looked at the bit left in his hand, shrugged and continued chewing, "It's good, thank you." He took another bite and a sip of water. The effect on Kyrie was instantaneous. A bright smile spread across her face.

After finishing the small bit of food, and all the water Kyrie had, Alex's shaking hands had calmed. "Why are you helping us?" Alex asked. A sudden thought hit him. "Wait," he grabbed Kyrie, "What happened to the other one who helped me? Is he okay?"

She immediately recoiled, and Chloe gently pried a terrified Kyrie from Alex's grip. Alex apologized immediately. "No, it is not your fault," Kyrie grimaced, "For too long we have been intimidated and kept in fear." She stood tall. "That is why I am here. I want to help you, and I hope," She met each one of their gazes in turn, "you will help us finally be free of Pryor and his evil."

"If there is anything we can do to end that bastard, I'm all for it," Aaron growled. "If we can help you in the process, so much the better."

"I will tell the others you are willing to help." Then sudden doubt-filled Kyrie's face.

"What?" Chloe asked.

"Many of us want freedom, but there are others I must convince."

"You tell us this *now*?" Aaron demanded. Anger burned in his eyes, like the flame in his hand.

"Calm down," Alex shouted.

"I will do what I can." Kyrie eyed the fire fearfully. "There is something you can do that will help, though."

"Defeat Alistair," Chloe interrupted. Kyrie nodded in acknowledgment and took Chloe's hand. Giving Alex and Aaron a nod of confidence, Kyrie turned to Norah.

"They will need the wolf." She held out a hand. Norah held her wolf protectively. "This is very important to me." She spoke more to the toy than the other woman. "Keep him safe?"

"I promise to protect him," Kyrie answered, taking the wolf from Norah's hesitant hand. A look passed between them, "Pryor will pay for what he has done," she assured them as she turned to go.

"It's time we put an end to Alistair," Aaron growled. Turning to Norah, he asked, "Can you find him?" Norah nodded and disappeared through the wall.

The Search

"That little bitch and her friends need to show themselves soon," Alistair complained. "Did you hear that?" He spun to stare at a space of the blank wall.

"You need to relax; my servants will find them." Pryor sighed.

"The same servants who just tried to kill you?" Alistair questioned, only to be ignored by Pryor.

"Then perhaps you should go out to find her. I will await your call if you need assistance." He smiled in a way that made Alistair want to destroy him. Biting back a retort and forcing calm, Alistair returned the smile.

He was five minutes away when he paused to think. Maybe the old bastard was right. As he descended the stairs, Alistair held out his hand, trying to feel remnants of magic. "This might be more trouble than it is worth, especially if that idiot's creatures have decided to help Chloe." Closing his eyes, he could feel the tingle of a spell caster who was trying to hide more than their magic. It felt like a very weak spell, cast by someone who hadn't practiced in a long time. Well, that was disappointing, Alistair thought. He was at least hoping for a challenge.

Following the trail of magic, Alistair found himself looking down a long dimly lit hall that ended in an operating theater. Here was where the spell caster was. Cocking his head to the side, he could feel something more, something powerful and ancient. Calling up energy, he tossed the ball of light into the air, letting it descend before him. Stopping, he held out a hand and he felt the air. "Oh, my my," Alistair laughed, feeling the power the magic left behind. "Not all gone, yet no longer as strong, but… something?" He paused, perplexed.

Shaking off the doubt, he resumed down the hall. Nearing the end, a wicked smile spread across his face. He could hear voices coming through the slightly open door. As soon as his hand rested on the door the voices stopped.

"We've been waiting for you, Alistair," Chloe called. The result was not what she had been hoping for. Pushing the door open, Alistair was laughing. He showed no signs of defense or the remotest of tension. He stood watching the four of them: Alex, who burned with demon hatred, Aaron, who readied spells far more advanced than last time, a giant ghost wolf, who growled menacingly… and darkness flowed around Chloe.

"Why do you stand there so defiant?" Alistair finally asked. "Are we not on the same side?" He ignored the stammered words and curses. "I am a sorcerer and you are half breeds, undead, and a magician." Even though he was trying to relate, he could not keep the disdain from his voice.

"You are a vile, disgusting creature, and we are nothing like you," Chloe spat. "Hell made a mistake when it let you escape. That is something I will not do."

Alistair sighed, "I will admit you are stronger than I originally thought you would be. However, you are still nothing compared to me." With a wave of his hand, he sent bolts of electricity flying. His calm cracked slightly when the energy was absorbed by Aaron. Alistair barely had time to create a shield before his attack was thrown back at him. "I tire of this," he shouted, throwing spells into the room. Quickly he conjured twenty minions; small hairless creatures. Their glowing eyes and sharp claws all aimed toward Chloe. They charged in.

Alex threw out his hands, sending many of the creatures flying. Aaron concentrated his spells against Alistair. Another wave of minions appeared, but these had wings. Chloe's anger grew, setting half of the flying evils aflame. Alistair conjured more little creatures, which began to crawl over each other to become a giant being. It lumbered into the room—straight into the jaws of Norah.

Confrontation

"Why should we help them?" A creature that seemed to be a cross between a bear and a large man, growled. A few other angry voices grumbled their agreement. Kyrie recoiled slightly from the anger.

"We can at least hear what she has to say," a rabbit man countered.

"Why? If we help them, then what? We are still trapped," a deer woman questioned. More and more voices joined the din.

Suddenly there was a great booming call for quiet. Kyrie, like many others, threw their hands over their ears. "I will have silence!" A giant boar known as Duartz limped up to Kyrie. One of his legs was part boar and part human, mismatched with his other human leg. The grumbling voices did not completely stop, but at least they were reduced to a murmur. Kyrie recoiled further as Duartz approached. His face and bare chest were covered in scars. He was one of the first to receive Dr. Pryor's treatments. He was slightly hunched over, his skin the color of sour milk, hanging loosely from his face and arms. He wore the same type of mismatched clothes as the others, the things left behind by patients, and clothes that had once belonged to the human versions of themselves. He gave Kyrie an appraising once over. "I believe I would like to hear why we should help, as well."

Kyrie wasn't sure what direction Duartz was leaning toward. His tone and face gave nothing away. Many others made it perfectly clear they did not want to have anything to do with her.

"Now is the time to strike," Kyrie called over the insults and protests. "Listen, these people can help us, they want to help us."

"Why?" A gruff voice called from the crowd. It held hope, apprehension, and no small amount of fear. Kyrie noticed several creatures begin to wander away in disgust.

"Humans don't care." "Or they want us dead." "If we do win, our kind won't accept us, and neither will the humans." Shouts agreed. "Without the doctor, how will we survive?" This was followed by shouts of "How will we eat?" and "Where will we live?"

They accosted Kyrie's ears. "We will live here!" Kyrie shouted, her breathing rising to match her anger.

Duartz stepped in front of her, glaring at the others. "How many of us are hunters?" he demanded. "We have the means and the knowledge."

Voices joined in a cacophony to drown out his words. Several more creatures turned from them. Kyrie had reached her limit. "I am going to help. I refuse to live as a slave any longer." Her words landed like a bomb. Deep in their hearts, they had known this, even though they had always been called servants.

"But, but, who will take care of Master?" a frightened voice asked. The speaker had not intended to be heard, but he chose the wrong time to speak.

Kyrie glared at them all. "Master, slave, it doesn't matter—you're all sheep."

"Hey!" a wooly face shouted angrily.

Ignoring the other's stunned looks, Kyrie stormed out. Halfway down the hall, the anger and adrenaline failed her. Shaking, falling against the wall, the weight of her words crashed over her. Taking a few deep breaths, she stood straight and shrugged. "Well, if I fail, I'll be dead anyway."

"That's the spirit," laughed a being with a face like a cougar, "Great confidence builder."

Behind the man were many of the semi-humans she had just shouted at. They were smiling tensely at her.

An explosion rocked the building. The smiles disappeared.

Testing

"Where the hell are all of these things coming from?" Alex demanded.

"They come from all around," Alistair laughed. "Rats, insects, lizards, I use them all."

One swipe of a huge paw covered the floor in streaks of blood. "No wonder there are so many." Norah cleared another swath through the attack.

Aaron threw an energy ball at Alistair, who brushed it aside as if it was fluff in the air. "You seemed to be getting tired," Alistair taunted.

Aaron glanced at Alex who was busy with the composite creature. Chloe and Norah destroyed wave after wave of small creatures. Another energy bolt flew to the side, exploding part of the wall. "We're not getting anywhere," Chloe shouted, her frustration growing. "I have had enough!" she shouted. A blast wiped out all the attacking creatures. Alistair was sent rocketing through the doors, knocking them from their hinges.

Alistair struggled, trying to get up. His eyes, which seconds before had held contempt, now shone with fear. His legs would not hold his weight.

Aaron fell to one knee, exhausted. Alex began to advance on the wizard but the flame that had surrounded him was burning low. Norah had returned to her human ghost form. Out of all of them, only Chloe seemed to be intensifying in her power. She turned tall, gaunt, and angry. She looked from Alex to Alistair.

"How dare you take him from me?" Chloe's harsh voice threatened. A wave of her hand sent the injured wizard smashing back into the wall. "How dare you threaten my family?" A deep gash cut across Alistair's chest. Blood cascaded over his shirt, drenching the material. "How dare you threaten me?!" His head snapped back, smashing against the wall, a wound opened across his cheek.

"How dare you kill Liza?!" Chloe's hand shot forward. Alistair gasped, and blood spurted over his lips. Alex cringed at the crunching and snapping of bones. Alistair's chest caved in, inch by inch, as each rib shattered. Alistair's eyes flew wide as his sternum exploded, along with his heart. The surprise, and life, left his eyes. Alistair's body twitched once, then twice.

Slowly Alistair's ghost rose from his body. Chloe watched as she began to shrink back to her normal size. He began to laugh, his hands lighting with magic. "You thought you could defeat me?"

Chloe stumbled back, and Alex pulled her into his arms. Norah resumed her wolf form, and the glint of Liza showed in Aaron's eyes. They braced to continue the battle.

Alistair howled when the fiery pit opened next to him. Kerlvin appeared, still holding the grumbling head of Simon. "Oh, my dear Alistair, your time is up." Kerlvin's clawed hand sunk into Alistair's leg. The wizard cried out, his hands clawing along the floor, as Kerlvin smiled at Chloe. "Always a pleasure. See you soon." The demon nodded to the exhausted group.

Alistair tried to fight. His spells struck harmlessly against Kerlvin, whose scales shone like red armor. He toyed with the wizard, acting as if there might be a chance of escape. "This was entertaining, but I grow bored." Flame engulfed the demon and screaming ghost. Alistair's screams were silenced when the pit closed.

Norah floated out to stare at the place where hell had opened. She squeaked her surprise.

Standing before several deformed and growling semi-humans stood Dr. Pryor. "Well, I thought he would never leave."

Results

"This has been a very enlightening few days." Pryor rubbed his hands together as he eyed the retreating ghost. "Demons, ghosts, wizards— oh so many new beings to explore!" Bending down, he inspected the corpse of Alistair. "Such a waste," he muttered, taking a syringe from his pocket.

"Stop him!" Norah shouted. Alex rushed forward, but he was blocked by one of Pryor's servants. Pryor held up the blood-covered needle. He eyed it, enraptured for a moment, before jamming it into his own vein. Norah's voice broke to a bark. A beast-man lunged at her. Then its body flew to the side, its throat torn out, blood spurting from the wound.

Norah's teeth chomped at Pryor's face, but were held just out of reach. The evil doctor observed the ghost wolf, his hand out in front of him, as he held her back with magic. Alex threw his demon rage at Pryor, only to have it brushed away.

"It seems like the demon blood is not as permanent as I had hoped." Flicking two fingers, he sent Alex flying across the room. Taping a sigil on his arm, Pryor glared at Chloe. She couldn't move for a second. Then one of Aaron's spells smashed into Pryor. Chloe nearly crumpled. Recovering, she ran to Alex. Holding him, she found that neither could move.

Pryor growled with pain and anger as he swatted at the flames burning the side of his face and shoulder. "Kill them!" he ordered. His beasts charged into the room. From the wall, Norah charged in wolf form. Bodies flew, filling the room with yelps and growls. Pryor tried to trap Aaron with the little magic he knew, only to have Aaron block him and counter with Liza's skill. Her voice came through Aaron's as he fought.

"You will never hurt another!" they shouted.

"Destroy that one first!" Pryor ordered his creatures. Several ran toward Aaron, while many more stood glaring at him. "I said, destroy him!" He pressed a sigil on his arm. The creatures who not obeying crumpled in agony. "Remember, I am your master—you must obey me!" He gouged his finger deeper into the renewed flesh of his arm. Howls of pain intensified.

Then they were drowned out by Pryor's own scream. His arm and other hand were both gone. Blood dribbled from his desiccated veins.

Chloe was free. Her anger swelled. The attacking semi-humans faltered under her glare. Several turned to run. Her rage could not be contained. Aaron slid behind her to shield Alex. Norah spit out the severed bits of Pryor as she leapt from the room.

Pryor's face lit in victory for an instant. Blood from his severed limbs began to shoot toward each other. Suddenly his arm, hand, and all the beast-men in the room vaporized. Chloe's terrible visage glared at him in triumph. Silence fell.

Pryor was aware of heavy breathing all around him. "Murderer," "Torturer," "Devil," they whispered their hate. It grew in intensity, turning into shouts. Pryor turned, moving as fast as his ancient body would carry him. His heart beat in panic, sending blood out of his severed arms in spurts. As he bled, the effects of Alistair's blood also drained away. Norah burst through a wall in front of him. He spun to face the semi-humans, his *failed* experiments, hateful glares.

Trapped between the giant wolf ghost and the advancing army of his own creation, the doctor ordered, threatened, and finally, begged. Chloe cringed at his awful, high-pitched wail of agony.

Pryor's screams ceased, leaving only growling and tearing. Alex blinked into consciousness. Chloe held him as Aaron cast a healing spell. They helped him to his feet. "They're both gone," Alex sighed.

Kyrie, nearby, nodded in affirmation. Norah's wolf form ducked back into the room. She returned to her normal size and form as she approached, her hand held out. Kyrie smiled as she returned the stuffed wolf named Horo. "Thank you for keeping him safe." Norah smiled.

Kyrie looked at the burnt remnants of the battle. "Thank you for helping us rid ourselves from the yoke of Dr. Pryor." She took a step toward Chloe with an outstretched hand. She stood firm and resolute. Chloe took her hand firmly.

Turning, Chloe pulled Norah into a tight embrace. "I still can't get used to you being able to do that," Norah smiled as Chloe released her, "but I wouldn't trade it for anything."

Chloe looked past Norah and asked, "Anything?"

Goodbye

Billy's transparent form stood in the doorway. Norah stared, speechless. "Norah?" he whispered.

"Billy?" She ran the distance between them, but stopped before his open arms, "Why now? Where were you? I needed you!"

"I'm so sorry; I wanted to help; I wanted to be here, but all I could do was watch." Tears were streaming down his face. He turned to the semi- humans watching him from the hall. "I could only watch. I wanted to help but I couldn't get in." He fell to his knees, his face buried in his hands. "I couldn't stop him from hurting any of you."

Norah's arms enveloped him. "It was too late to save me," she soothed him.

"But you were so alone, I wanted to be here for you." He wept.

She held Horo out to him. "You were." She lifted his chin to smile at him.

"You were always so kind." "Thank you for taking care of us." Several of the semi-humans spoke their appreciation.

"I think you can go now." Chloe nodded to the wall behind them. Alex smiled at what he saw, then laughed as Aaron grumbled.

"I can't see anything. What?" Liza spoke in Aaron's mind, and suddenly he could see what they saw. "Oh, there it is, thanks."

Billy got slowly to his feet as he held out his hand. "Hey Norah," he smiled, "I think it is this way." He pointed to a huge area behind him, where the wall disappeared. Through the gap, they could see a long road leading to wide, rolling green hills. Norah hesitated, until she glanced up at his face. He seemed older, kinder, at peace.

Norah took a step toward him, eyes squinting. Then she smiled slowly. As they all watched, Norah seemed to grow. She took a step toward Billy, then paused and cocked her head to the side. "What is that way?"

Billy's smile faltered slightly, but it came back quickly. "Our parents. I think. A new life?" He looked over his shoulder. "I think we can go home." He turned around, holding out a hand to her. Her smile grew wider as she moved closer. Suddenly she stopped turned around and ran to Chloe. Tears glistened in her eyes as she smiled and laughed.

"I'm going *home!*" She grabbed Chloe, pulling her into a hug. Chloe held the young girl in her arms. She could feel the hope emanating from her. Norah broke the hug, turned, ran three steps, turned around, ran back and pushed something into Chloe's hands, then ran back, taking Billy's hand. They stared at each other for a few moments before turning and heading down the road.

Norah turned back once to wave before the portal disappeared.

Chloe laughed as a tear rolled down her cheek. Alex pulled her tight around the shoulder. She smiled wider as she held out the small stuffed wolf to him. Alex looked, and then he spied Kerlvin. He had appeared at the place where the portal had been. The demon brushed something from his eye. He saw Alex watching him, and he disappeared.

"That couldn't have happened soon enough," Aaron muttered. "Can we go home now?"

"Yes, please." Alex agreed as his stomach growled. "Although I wouldn't say no to more jerky." He looked at Kyrie hopefully, but she shook her head sadly.

Epilogue

Chloe and Alex visited Saint Mary's whenever they were in the area., which wasn't as often as they would have liked. Sadly, Fear the cat and Oliver the ghost cat had decided to take up residence in the former hospital.

The semi-humans, led by Kyrie and the old boar Duartz, had done a fantastic job of making the place nice and habitable. They were a new kind of creature, neither fully human nor fully beast, but they had a community now. Aaron, with Liza's knowledge, had cast an enchantment that prevented almost all visitors from wanting to find or enter the place.

There was only one problem, Kyrie noted, as she surveyed the comfortable common room. It had originally been the lobby. The beautiful red couch never seemed to be free of fur, but that was not the issue. She looked at the windows of the doors leading to the connecting hall. An ugly glaring face stared back. Kyrie knew the ghost of Linda was spewing words of hate at her. Kyrie sighed. It would be nice to be able to use the hallway. "But it is not worth the annoyance," she told her close friend Walter, and the cougar-man nodded his agreement as they took the long way to the upper floors.

***

Chloe retrieved the mail. She read over the postcard Aaron had sent from Scotland, then turned her attention to a small package. "Alex, there is a package for you from Kyrie," Chloe called. Alex rushed to take the box from her hands. She shook her head and smiled as Alex sighed contentedly, and his eyes rolled in bliss as he chewed his annual treat of squirrel jerky.